BLOOD
CHIT

For Bill Hopkins,
Fellow VET & Fellow Author —
Thank You for Your Service!

Grady Smith

BLOOD
CHIT

A Novel

Grady Smith

APC
Apippa Publishing Company
Riverdale Park, Maryland

First edition, 2012.
Visit Gradysmithbooks.com for additional news and information.

Library of Congress Control Number: 2011942105

Smith, Grady A.

Blood Chit/Grady Smith. 1st ed.

ISBN: 978-0-9798992-2-5

1. Fiction   2. Vietnam War   3. Post-Traumatic Stress Disorder (PTSD)

ATTENTION CORPORATIONS, UNIVERSITIES, COLLEGES, AND PROFESSIONAL ORGANIZATIONS: Quantity discounts are available on bulk purchases of this book for educational purposes, fundraising, or gift-giving. Contact APC, P.O. Box 54, Riverdale Park, MD 20738

Manufactured in the United States of America.

"You come from a family of Samurai," Kabuo's father said to him in Japanese. "Your great-grandfather died because he could not stop being one."

Snow Falling on Cedars
David Guterson

VIETNAM

Chapter 1

"Rattlesnake definitely does not taste like chicken, not for my money," Captain Bonner said. He paused a second to build a little suspense. "Oh, but now *alligator*," he said, smacking his lips, "that's real succulent critter."

He got a nice laugh from his captive audience of three. They stood in a semicircle around him—Chaplain McCurdy, the Warrant Officer pilot, Garrett Prue, and Staff Sergeant Chuck Paxton.

"The night we had our survival meal in flight school," Mister Prue said, "they gave us a live goat to kill." They were standing beside his helicopter, and he paused a second to listen to a radio transmission. Then he went on. "The NCO in charge picked a city kid to cut its throat. I think the wildest animal he'd ever seen was a pink poodle," he said, and gave a swishy little gesture that got a chuckle. "He got his bayonet in the goat's neck but couldn't find the jugular. That poor goat— what a racket. We finally put it out of its misery. Skinned it, cut it up and roasted it."

"Hey, Padre," Captain Bonner said to Chaplain McCurdy. "Would you say grace over the goat or give it the last rites?"

"Both," the Chaplain replied. "*And* say prayers to ward off indigestion." Everybody laughed.

During the general laughter, Sergeant Paxton slid in beside the priest. "Hey, Padre," he said quietly. "Got a minute?" McCurdy gave him one of his patented Irish grins. "Sure. Come on," he said, and they walked about 20 feet away.

The company of ten slicks, Huey helicopters used to transport troops, had flown in a few minutes before and lined up in the field in staggered trail, a kind of symmetrical zigzag. When an artillery mission ended, they'd lift Captain Bonner's infantry company into its objective area. Not far away, two Cobras, the new helicopter gunships, waited to give fire support to the slicks at their landing zone, if it was needed.

The field where they were waiting sat next to the Nha Be tank farm on the banks of the Saigon River, just southeast of the capital. Two nights before, an NVA squad a kilometer or so away had dropped half-a-dozen quick rounds down a mortar tube and fled, leaving one of the storage tanks of crude blazing furiously. Now, although oily black smoke still rose from it, the tank was just about burned out.

"I need to go to confession, Padre," Paxton said to the priest. The noise of the Hueys ensured privacy.

"As soon as I got here, I gave general absolution to everybody going out on the lift. It's a combat zone privilege, comes with being shot at, so you're covered." Chaplain McCurdy gave him another grin.

"Yeah, but I kind of scared myself last night."

Padre's face grew serious. McCurdy knew that, over Paxton's ten months in country, the sergeant had developed into the strongest squad leader in the company. Which brought disadvantages.

"What happened?"

"I was with one of the girls at Mama Huong's." His eyes faltered just a bit, then sought the priest's as he went on. "And when I was done, I looked at her. There was so much hate in her face you could feel the vibrations. And that pissed me off so bad I almost..." He stopped, frightened by the recollection. "I've never been that mad in my life. I wanted to...it was all I could do to keep from hitting her. With my fist." He dropped his voice, appalled by the memory. "I wanted to kill her, I really did."

"Well, remember, getting shot at does funny things to people sometimes—not just soldiers but civilians, too, including prostitutes. She can blame all the destruction on us, even her condition in life. And when a troop's been over here awhile, he can buy into that with guilt. And that changes into a tremendous amount of anger, as you found out. After lust, anger's the sin I hear most about in confession. Anger and hate."

That surprised Paxton. "Not fear?"

"Listen," the priest responded, "when somebody out there wants to kill you, fear's not a sin, it's a survival skill." Paxton smiled for a second but didn't feel any better. "Let me give you absolution anyway, just to make it official." And he did, carving out the sign of the cross. Paxton mirrored it by crossing himself, but he still looked haunted by the incident at Mama Huong's.

"Hey," Padre said. "When do you fly away from this green sauna?"

That brought a grin that stayed around a bit. "Seventeen May, nineteen and sixty-eight," he said, and actually chuckled.

"Wow," Padre said. "You're out of here in two months."

"Fifty-six days, Padre. Fifty-six and a wakeup." Padre clapped him on the shoulder and they headed back to Captain Bonner and Mister Prue.

"Sounds like you guys got the same survival course in flight school they gave us grunts," Bonner was saying.

"Yeah, but of course a whole bunch of flying stuff, too," Mister Prue explained. "Like how to get a shot-up helicopter back on the ground so you can walk away from it."

3

"What do you do?" Paxton was clearly interested.

"Well, if the engine conks out, you usually auto-rotate in. Or, you try to steer so you'll hit a tree or a building that looks like it'll break up easy. That can absorb a lot of the shock, and hopefully you'll be able to walk away from it."

"I used to feel pretty safe in these things," Paxton said.

"It's just immediate action drill, like what you do if you're caught in the kill zone of an ambush. You get an enormous amount of technical helicopter stuff, too. Oh, and you get this."

Mister Prue pulled out a piece of cloth about eight inches by fifteen. "This is my blood chit." Paxton closed in around him, curious. "It's a message in the language of every country or tribe you could possibly wind up in. It started out as an Air Force item, but we carry them now, too."

Paxton peered intently over his shoulder. The top third had a full-color American flag, and under it he counted 14 different versions of the message. Besides English, French and Dutch, it had Vietnamese, Thai, Burmese and two kinds of Chinese. A lot of the others, though they were named, meant nothing to him. He had no idea what countries or tribes spoke some of the languages. He read the English:

> I am a citizen of the United States of America. I do not speak your language. Misfortune forces me to seek your assistance in obtaining food, shelter and protection. Please take me to someone who will provide for my safety and see that I am returned to my people. My government will reward you.

"It's like an IOU for the help you get," Paxton said.

"That's exactly what it is," Mister Prue responded. "'I owe you for my life.' It's supposed to work like a traveler's check, so you don't have to assault unsuspecting goats."

"What do you do if the bad guys get hold of it?" Chaplain McCurdy asked.

Paxton gave a little laugh. "Pray they can't read."

✺

Paxton turned away from Captain Bonner. "This isn't right." The words came softly, as if he was talking to himself.

"What?" Bonner asked, smiling, not having understood.

Paxton turned back. "It isn't right." First Sergeant Jasper Hite took a step closer to the two, his eyes contracting to a pair of angry brown slashes in a sunburned face.

"What's not right?" Bonner asked.

"This is the third daylight patrol my squad's had in ten days. I had casualties in both the others. There's eight other rifle squads in the company, and some of them have never been out. It's not right."

"You shut up, Paxton, and just do it." The First Sergeant was holding on tightly to his flaring temper. "Get your sorry ass moving."

"I'm going, First Sergeant, but it's not right."

Bonner interrupted as the First Sergeant was about to unload. "Hang on, Top." He turned to Paxton. "I know you've been out there a lot, but this one's pretty important. That's why they told me to send my best squad leader."

Paxton was appalled. "You mean my people are going back out there again because of *me?*" Bonner subsided momentarily at the failure of his crude flattery.

"That's enough, Paxton." The First Sergeant bit off his words. "You get your people their extra rations and ammo, and move them out through third platoon at 0730." He looked at his watch. "That's 17 minutes."

"We'll make our departure time," Paxton said, standing at the tent flap. "But it's not right." And he was gone.

The First Sergeant scowled. "That sorry..."

"He's been doing some heavy lifting, but it hasn't been that bad," Bonner said.

"It's for you to say and him to do, sir. That's why they call it a chain of command."

"Yeah, but he's right—he's had three of his people killed or wounded his last couple of times out. And if he *thinks* he's got a problem ..."

"My heart pumps piss," said the First Sergeant.

⋇

Paxton moved quickly back toward his squad. For the first time since he'd been in country, he felt like Captain Bonner wasn't squaring with him. "Send your best squad leader"— Paxton knew what he was downwind from. First the flattery, then another recon mission. As he thought about it, he realized that's how Bonner did it the last two patrols. *How many more casualties today?* The hell with it—I'm mister short timer. *But it's wrong.*

Wrong or not, MACV Headquarters was still a mass of twitching nerve ends and chewed nails from the NVA's Tet offensive last month. General Westmoreland was all aquiver in his highly polished combat boots, wondering if the bad guys were going to do it again. And maybe they would.

But third squad had humbler, more immediate worries. Paxton and his people would be heading out in a matter of minutes and he needed to get his head on straight. He'd be working directly for the Old Man, Captain Bonner, on this patrol. Paxton would take his squad south for five kilometers to check out a stand of nipa palm that followed a nameless stream for another three clicks. Last night, airborne sensors picked up unusual readings in the area—at least 20 people, probably more, in two or three clumps. The main trunk of the Ho Chi Minh Trail wasn't that far west and the NVA could logger some much larger troop formations at the site on their way down from the north.

He gazed out at the terrain. For the last two days, large stretches of open rice paddies had lain in every direction, dotted with clumps of nipa palm. The open paddies would make their concealment on the march difficult, and sometimes impossible. The thick groves of nipa stalks, standing 20 or more feet high and clustered together in groves in the soft mud of tidal streams, would give the enemy plenty of cover. To work. His squad was short by five people and he talked his platoon sergeant out of Casey Jones, a grenadier from second squad. The tall, broad-chested black from Cairo, Illinois had been drafted right out of a lackluster four years in high school and found the discipline of the Army a pleasant revelation. Recognition based on performance and pay based on rank, not race, left a deep impression on him. He intended to make it a career. The other squad leader grumphed and humphed about temporarily losing Casey, but Paxton was satisfied. Seven was just about the right size for a recon patrol. Any less and there'd be too little firepower to break contact in a crunch and haul ass. Many more and you might as well announce yourself with a bullhorn.

Paxton's was the lightest squad in the platoon right now, but everybody was under strength. His platoon was down 15 men, but when his lieutenant complained to Captain Bonner, the Old Man was loud and clear about his own shortages. Bonner was concerned about taking fewer than a hundred soldiers on an operation. He said Roman centurions used to have a hundred men—"that's what the name meant," he explained, "honcho of a hundred troops"—and he ought to be taking at least 150 soldiers to the field. Replacements had been promised for two weeks.

When Paxton told his people they were going out on another daylight recon patrol, they took the news in silence. Gomez wouldn't make eye contact with him for a couple of minutes and looked intently at his boots. Paxton hoped nobody would hear about the Old Man's best squad leader bullshit.

"Okay, people," Paxton said, "today's mission." Gomez finally got in motion and pulled a small notebook out of his breast pocket to take down details. "Move ASAP five clicks to the recon area, avoid open paddies by using the nipa groves for concealment whenever we can. Check out the recon area to see why they got high infrared readings last night. Watch out for booby traps—when we were down there six weeks ago, there were some old ones. Now we could find a new bunch." Chain of command: Paxton, Patrol Leader. Al Gomez, Assistant Patrol Leader, and then Ken Janowitz. "Welcome back from R and R." Paxton grinned at Ken, who merely shrugged. "After Ken, it's whoever can get to the prick 25 and call for help." That got a smile or two, though not from Kessler, who carried one of the PRC-25 radios: "This lump on my back says, 'shoot me here.'" Kessler had arrived in country almost ten months earlier, a week or so after Paxton, and for virtually the whole time he'd been the squad leader's RTO. Now, with the end of their year's tour in sight, the two of them had begun talking cautiously about what they would do when they got back home.

Ken Janowitz didn't smile at Paxton's PRC-25 joke any more than Kessler. Five months before, as a newly arrived PFC in a sharp firefight, he'd found himself the closest functioning GI to the radio and coolly adjusted artillery fire to within a hundred meters of the American position. "Scrotum the size of a duffel bag," Captain Bonner said. With only a month in country, Janowitz found himself with a Bronze Star, Purple Heart and an instant promotion. In Nam, that kind of initiative was coin of the realm.

After Paxton briefed the mission, he and Gomez did the household chores. One extra C ration per man. Casey Jones said, "Give me ham and lima beans and my maximum effective range is out of sight." He got some chuckles and a few sidebar comments about any soldier who would actually *eat* ham and lima beans. Verify two full canteens of water per man, purification tablets added. Ammo, first-aid pouches, an extra battery for each of the two radios, insect repellent to flush off the leeches. "But don't use the repellent—or cigarettes," he said, looking straight at Schiller draping machine gun ammo diagonally across his chest, "until the chopper's inbound. Otherwise, the smell could put us in a crack."

He passed out the checkpoints they would have to call in, so the Old Man would know where they were. And the artillery registration points, so they wouldn't have to figure out their location as a six-digit grid coordinate before they could call in a fire mission. And the location of Landing Zone Cody— one of the slicks lifting out the company would break away and come for them there.

"Questions?" None. He looked at them—Gomez returned the notebook to his breast pocket. Kessler was doing a radio check with the Old Man's RTO. Janowitz was charging one last magazine with ammo. Casey Jones stowed the contents of his C ration box in his pack, while Schiller sucked on one last cigarette before they left the company perimeter. Mingo Sanders sat quietly, waiting for the word to move out. Paxton gave it to them: "Saddle up!"

He took the point himself at first, moving them out smartly to put as much distance between them and the rest of Bonner's company as fast as he could. To the NVA, the full company had to be about as quiet as a freight train and that suited Paxton just fine. With a distraction like that, he'd have a better chance of infiltrating his recon area without being detected. It was better going in on foot than by helicopter. He hated a single-chopper insertion on a mission like this because every NVA around would know where he was and that he only had as many soldiers as one slick could carry.

In the initial segment across open paddies, he spread his people out. Al Gomez, a solidly built Chicano with a wife and two daughters in Austin, Texas, brought up the rear. Al would keep his eye on Ted Schiller, a good man in a firefight with his

M60 machine gun, though he had a tendency to daydream on the commute to work. His six foot, two inch frame usually made people think basketball, but in the showers his long torso and highly developed upper body marked him as a swimmer back in Michigan's peninsula.

Paxton kept them well away from the dikes and in the paddies. They were more likely to come up with leeches and maybe some foot rot. It also shaved a little off their speed. But when the NVA set up their booby traps, they catered to GIs who walked high and dry, begging to have a foot blown off. He glanced back momentarily. Dispersion was good. Casey Jones was in the middle of the paddy doing a visual check on the nipa palm half a click to his left. Lima beans made good soldiers. He smiled.

As they got within small-arms range of the tree line they were making for, Paxton slowed the pace. The terrain ahead started the final leg of their approach to the recon area, but if there were any NVA in that vegetation they could shred the patrol up pretty good. He moved them with hand signals into a line abreast, maintaining dispersion. Then he pulled Schiller and his machine gun directly to his right. He wanted to be able to control the M60's fire, if he needed it. But no NVA opened up on them. Just inside the tree line, he put them in an outward-facing circle for a brief rest. ▮

The sun was well up now. Their pace had brought a good sweat, and they were all sucking on their canteens.

"Go easy on the water," he whispered to them. "Save some for later." He looked over at Kessler, screwing the cap back on his canteen. "Hey, Matt, what flavor?"

Matt Kessler got packets of pre-sweetened Kool-Aid in the mail from his mother. Paxton couldn't decide which was worse, the strong-arm taste of the purification tablets or the sticky, artificial fruit flavor Kessler would use to kill the taste of the medication. But Kessler had no doubts. "Goofy grape," he whispered back. Everyone grinned, except Casey Jones from second squad. Ken Janowitz explained the joke to him and he smiled too.

"Listen up, now," Paxton said. "We'll be in the recon area in less than five minutes. Start looking for booby traps on tree trunks and remember to check the stalks of nipa palm." He thought a second. "Look for anything that would show they were in here last night."

He walked about ten feet away and urinated, looking as he did for the booby traps he'd reminded his squad about. Then he moved them out, still in a scattered pattern but less widely dispersed inside the nipa palm. They advanced more slowly, their heads and eyes always in motion—checking where their next three paces would fall, the nearest tree trunk, the space they had to pass through between two stalks of nipa palm. Looking farther ahead, they did an eyeball sweep of the ground, then straight ahead, then above. And back, side, and forward to maintain visual contact with the others.

The second grenadier, Mingo Sanders, slightly built with warm, brown skin, held up his right hand to call a halt. Gingerly, he approached a two-man pit in the earth a dozen feet away. He toed the dirt around its lip and found it relatively dry, then peered into it. He mouthed the word 'old' to Paxton and put his hand at his knee to indicate how deep the water was in the hole. Digging in paddy country like this, you could hit the water table well before a foxhole was deep enough to hunker down in. But any NVA would gladly put up with a wet behind rather than leave his head hanging out in the shrapnel scatter of a 500-pound bomb. They moved on.

Positions showed up more frequently but checked out several months old. They came across an old booby trap tied to a tree, improvised from plastic explosive with bits of metal pressed into it, and molded around a blasting cap that was now inert. The field expedient hand grenade had once been connected to a tripwire set at about shin height between two trees, but the wire was missing. If the entire company was here they'd likely blow it in place, but given the strength of their patrol they didn't need to do that kind of advertising. Paxton pointed it out to Kessler, who alerted Gomez. Everybody else skirted around it at a respectful distance.

On the other side of the stream they were following, they glimpsed some huts. That meant they were officially in their recon area. Paxton halted the patrol and walked over to Kessler, who gave him the handset. He keyed the push-to-talk button and very softly said, "Wonder six, Rover three one. Checkpoint red." After a second he got a terse "Roger."

Paxton waved them across the stream so they could check out the huts. On his left, Janowitz took two steps and stopped in his tracks, softly snapping his fingers. He was pointing at something where an old path led to the water. When Paxton got there, he found an olive drab anti-personnel mine. This was no field expedient—storebought was his term, and it was newly installed.

They were not alone.

Whoever was out there, they were fresh. Still having their basic issue of these Anti-Personnel mines meant they were just down from the north. Infantry probably, or maybe engineers, numbers unknown. It depended on their mission. He went from soldier to soldier to pass along this new cautionary information. He walked with a sharpened respect, almost a reverence, for the power to kill that lurked in the land.

He thought of the enemy in two separate tiers, troops and terrain. In point of fact, the terrain was neutral, a friend of the side controlling it. But you couldn't control it all the time or even very much of it most of the time. So, no matter how often you'd been over a piece of ground, when you went in cold you had to assume it was the enemy. And like right now, you weren't very often disappointed. The trick was to turn the tables and make the terrain your friend with your own booby traps and mines, and with night artillery of harassing and interdicting fires. Enemy troops, of course, couldn't ever be turned into friends, but every now and then they proved to be stupid, which was almost as good.

They resumed crossing the stream, pushing over into the eastern portion of the nipa grove. Janowitz and Sanders went first, then Paxton, Kessler, and Schiller with the machine gun, and finally Jones and Al Gomez. Paxton deployed them just inside the concealment of the wood line in a way that would let their fire cover both the front and rear of the clutch of buildings, then he crossed the 15 meters of open paddy to the back of the nearest hut.

He'd been here before, almost two months ago. And this time, as before, he found no nasty surprises crossing over. At the back of the hut, he carefully made a small opening in the thatch and peered in. The mud-wattle bomb shelter was still intact in the middle of the hut. The area was close enough to the Ho Chi Minh Trail to invite an occasional stick of bombs from the B52s on night delivery. Apparently, the shelter hadn't been enough protection and the families living in these huts had abandoned them. He saw some fresh military wrappings inside the doorway, maybe from those storebought mines, and a bit of leftover chow. Oh, that welcome stupidity, which never failed to make Paxton feel savvy, like the Most Experienced Person Present. Some NVA had left the stuff clearly visible to anyone at the door of the hooch. Paxton decided a second lieutenant was in charge, or a new sergeant right out of NCO academy. He was beginning to feel downright cocky when his eye picked up the tripwire across the doorway, an inch off the ground. They had baited their hook with the military garbage, trolling for GI dummies, and they almost got one. He revised his opinion of the NVA sappers, while the surge of adrenaline dissipated. Were they expecting

13

U.S. troops, but not quite this soon? And where were they, anyway?

Back in the nipa, he briefed the patrol members again. Everybody had to be kept up to speed on what they'd found, so they'd know what to look for while they walked their walk. Also, if the patrol was hit and only one or two made it out, they had to know everything the patrol leader knew. Otherwise, the effort and the casualties would be thrown away for nothing.

They continued south through the hostile terrain. At once they began to find fresh positions, with soil around the top still damp—old ones renewed, others quite recently dug. But there were no more booby traps. Those seemed limited to the outer perimeter of the new positions.

Halfway down their mission area, the stream split. In the crotch stood three older abandoned huts, much more dilapidated. Paxton sent Al Gomez to check them, but there were no baited hooks. He got a laconic "roger" when he reported checkpoint yellow.

Then he set the patrol in an outward-facing circle while they ate. When he was digging a small hole to bury his garbage, he came across a bit of old NVA trash—some rusting ends of commo wire and a few food wrappers—and wondered what the archaeologists would make of all these layers a hundred years from now. The can for Casey Jones' ham and lima beans would probably be a footnote in somebody's book.

They were done in less than fifteen minutes. He stood and gave them the infantryman's mantra: "Saddle up."

Although the west fork of the stream technically wasn't part of his mission, he sent Casey Jones and Ken Janowitz far enough to verify that the positions down that leg hadn't been improved. They found a storebought AP mine and came back. The mine, Paxton decided, marked the outer perimeter of the NVA positions at that point.

14

He made some quick calculations. If the rest of their recon area had the same density of newly prepared positions that they'd found so far, the NVA could shoehorn as much as a regiment in here. Whoever was preparing these positions would guide them in through the ring of booby traps at the north end, probably in the next night or two. Then they'd funnel out the bottom along the east fork of the stream and be facing straight toward the underbelly of Saigon. They could seriously disrupt business at the Cholon post exchange for a couple of days. Paxton's job now was to check the rest of his area and then get his patrol out as unobtrusively as he could, so the NVA regiment would stick to its plan. Then, when the sensors got the right readings, the B52s would bomb this whole area, and artillery would follow up with concentrations on their likely withdrawal routes.

They pushed on along the east fork of the stream. The density of the improved positions remained constant. When Gomez checked out a group of five more abandoned huts in the paddies east of the nipa palm, he found one with a repeat of the trash and booby trap arrangement. The huts were also designated checkpoint green. Paxton nodded to Kessler to call it in. But where were the damned NVA?

These latest huts, marking the official end of his recon area, stood at the extreme upper left of an open rice paddy half a kilometer square, flat as a checkerboard, and without so much as a bush sticking up above the top of the dikes. This open expanse was also designated LZ Cody and their slick would pick them up out in the middle, but closer to the bottom end where the nipa groves began coming together to form an open-ended V. They continued on until the stream brought them to the lower edge of the open area. The only tricky part would be finding a route through the perimeter between the inevitable booby traps. Tricky, yes, but also exhilarating and almost fun. He knew his squad would locate the storeboughts and navigate through them, and in two hours he'd be standing under a hot shower back at base camp. He called in "LZ Cody" to let the Old Man know they were ready to move out onto the pickup zone. They'd get the word to go when the bird was five minutes out.

He mulled over the meticulous preparation of all those positions they'd found, threw in the storebought AP mines, and decided he was tracking engineers rather than infantry—probably a platoon. Plausible, yes, but where the hell were they? They probably finished up here and moved on to the next bivouac site, but they'd have to leave guides behind to get the main body through the APs. Well, just so they don't try to seriously disrupt our extraction out on the LZ, he thought. It would be the ultimate stupidity if they did, but something an inexperienced engineer platoon leader might try. Artillery and TAC air would clean their clocks good, but they could do a number on Paxton's patrol before he could get the fire support cranked up.

He took Mingo Sanders with him scouting their route onto Cody. They located three fresh AP mines—two buried, rigged to detonate when stepped on, the third about seven or eight feet up in the vegetation and attached to a tripwire strung along the ground. Its explosion at that level would have something like the effect of an artillery round set for height-of-burst, detonating a specified distance above the ground and scattering its whirling steel fragments onto the enemy below. It was devastating against troops in open areas, and there were lots of those in the vast sprawl of the delta. Even Sanders with his little M79 grenade launcher could use the technique by aiming his round, about the diameter of a silver dollar or so, into overhanging branches above a dug-in position. The serrated wire wrapped around its inner charge would shatter into hundreds of tiny metallic splinters and whirl down on the soldiers below. It was a good trick for a grenadier to know.

Then, Paxton got a diabolical little idea that brought a smile to his face. The tripwire for the mine in the tree extended out from the left side of the trunk, the side that was more tramped down. Guides would bring the NVA through on the right side in the dark. If he could re-string the tripwire across the less worn side, he could take out a few bad guys. At the same time, he'd turn the ground into U.S. terrain—for the simple reason that they couldn't be sure whether the engineer platoon leader screwed up or Americans had come in and messed with it. So, they'd have to treat it like every square inch had been reverse booby-trapped. He liked that.

First, he told Sanders to get some more distance, then he started quickly to work. The trick was to keep the tension constant on the tripwire. He tied it down temporarily to the root where it right-angled from vertical to horizontal. Next, he freed the running end from its terminal anchor. Then he began resetting it on the right side.

Sanders' jaw dropped open when he realized what Paxton was up to.

"Goddam, Sarge," he said. "You want to get your face blown off?"

Paxton was sweating freely now and enjoying it. He grinned at Sanders. He was already into some kind of high—his rapid pulse told him that, and the funny taste he got in his mouth whenever he worked with explosives. The biggest pucker was freeing the tripwire after the running end was re-tethered. The tension had to duplicate what was there when he started. He got on the side of the tree away from the mine. Then he reached around for the end of the cord he'd used to tie down the tripwire. Slowly, he drew it along until the cord, backtracking on itself, pulled through its own last loop and the knot vanished. No explosion.

Then, he heard Kessler's low whistle. He and Sanders moved back fast to the radio.

"ETA zero five," Kessler said. Except that a minute had already gone by, so the bird was four minutes out.

"Saddle up, saddle up!" But they'd heard Kessler on the horn and had already shrugged back into their packs. "What heading?"

"Zero zero zero," Kessler replied. So the bird would be coming in due north, even though that would give it a light crosswind. Terrain drove that. They didn't want to be coming in across a place of concealment for the bad guys, like the trees, or lose track of altitude for a split second in the face of enemy machine gun fire and snag a skid in a treetop.

"Three anti-personnels at the tree line, two in the ground, one overhead. Follow me through in single file. When we hit the paddies, spread out. Maintain dispersion." He looked at his watch. Three minutes. "Let's move out."

He set off at an easy trot, slouching a bit forward to counterbalance his pack. Kessler was right on his heels with the radio. The pilot would come up on the command push momentarily. He took them left of the mine in the tree, pointing up at it without turning or breaking stride, then they cleared the tree line and splashed into the paddies.

"Spread out, stay off the dikes," Paxton said in a normal voice.

Once they could be seen, he felt it didn't much matter if they were heard. It wasn't that he shouted, but it always relieved some of the tension for him to be able to talk out like that. They pushed straight east and made good headway through the water, taking a bit less than two minutes to reach the approximate middle of the open area. As they sloshed along, the noise reminded Paxton momentarily of kids in a pool, but instead of laughing and yelling there was only their hard breathing. At the midpoint he turned them sharply left and continued moving northward because the closeness of the opposite tree line made him uncomfortable. Those trees could hide anything, but they angled away to the east, so the farther north he went the more distance he got from them. Then he heard the whop-whop-whop of the helicopter.

"Rover three-one, this is Eagle two-seven. Pop smoke." Paxton slowed and reached around for a smoke grenade hanging on his pack. Kessler passed him at full speed and Paxton heard him, breathing hard, gasp out a "roger" as he pulled the pin and tossed the grenade onto a paddy dike. The whop-whop-whop was louder. They'd see the chopper any second. At the soft pop of the grenade, Kessler turned and glanced back at the vivid yellow smoke starting to rise and spoke into his handset. "Smoke out." Paxton, 20 feet back, turned and held up his hand to halt the patrol, then picked up his pace to catch up with the radio.

"Hey, Kessler," he yelled, "this is the place!"

Kessler stopped, grinning. Out of breath, he looked back over his shoulder and gave a little toss of his head to signal he had heard. Then there was a deafening explosion from very close in front of him, and a wall of heat and a massive shock wave picked him up and threw him bodily into Paxton, rolling them together in a tangle in the filthy paddy water. Through the intense ringing in his ears, Paxton could hear brisk small-arms fire. They were dead center of sector in an ambush, and Kessler was screaming. But when he looked down, the two of them wrapped together, he saw that the entire left side of Kessler's head was a jumbled mess of ripped flesh and bone fragments and brain matter, with only hacked-up remnants of his ear remaining and his eye completely vanished. And then Paxton realized he was the one who was screaming.

He wrenched the handset from Kessler's grasp, forcing himself to ignore the unidentifiable bloody shreds plastered to it. "Hot LZ! Hot LZ!" When the roger came back, he was already pulling the radio off Kessler's body, the rounds from enemy automatic fire snapping just overhead. The slick was well short of their position and already executing a hard left-hand turn. But the bird had come escorted, and two Cobra gunships were getting ready to roll in for a firing pass on the enemy positions.

Prone in the paddy 30 feet behind Paxton and to his right, Sanders was struggling toward the dike for cover, holding his M79 above the water with his left hand while his right arm dangled uselessly. The handset for the second radio, which Sanders carried, dragged through the water at the end of its cord. Paxton scooped up Kessler's radio by its shoulder straps and ran, bent double, to the same dike Sanders was making for, followed all the way by the snap of enemy rounds right behind him. An NVA machine gun's location in the tree line was obvious from the rhythmic streaks of green tracers coming across at them a foot above the water. And there were four unseen rounds for every one that showed green.

"Schiller, get that machine gun!" But Schiller was already sending a stream of his own orange tracers into the nipa. As Paxton ran to Sanders, Schiller began to draw AK47 fire and Gomez, just beyond Schiller's machine gun, squeezed off ten quick rounds of semi-automatic trying to suppress the AKs.

Then the gunships were rolling in one behind the other and laying down rocket and machine-gun fire along the eastern tree line and just inside it, finally pulling up and away a hundred feet off the ground. Incredibly, the flat green trajectories continued in the face of the heavy fire from the helicopters, lifting and arcing up toward the gunships. Most of the strings of green lagged behind them, but one of the strands intersected the last gunship for a second or two. At once, small licks of flame sprang up from the engine housing on top of the ship. It shuddered visibly in midair and seemed to hesitate for a split second. Then it tipped over into a slow-motion plummet, the entire superstructure rotating in increasingly wild and erratic loops around an invisible axis in front of it, like some giant maple seed gone berserk. It crashed head first 60 feet north of Paxton, rolled over onto its side in a foot of paddy water, and lay still.

Paxton's first instinct was to help the two men in the downed gunship, but he squelched it ruthlessly. Instead, he ran to Sanders and grabbed the handset of his radio and half dragged, half carried him the rest of the way to the paddy dike. This radio was on the artillery Fire Direction Center's frequency, but he took one look and threw the handset down in frustration. A round had penetrated the PRC-25 on the side and exited at the middle of its broad back.

"Fuck," he said, quietly but with deep feeling, and turned to Kessler's radio. It was picking up a transmission. "Rover 31, this is Wonder 6. Tell me what's going on out there." Captain Bonner could hear the firefight five kilometers away and probably already had the company on the march toward their patrol.

"Help me out of this thing, will you?" Sanders was struggling one-handed to get the dead radio off.

He ignored the Old Man and Sanders both and changed the frequency on Kessler's radio to the Fire Direction Center's.

"Sarge!" It was Schiller. "Getting low on ammo."

"Well, ease back!" *Dumb shit.* Then, into the handset, "Peacock five, this is Rover three one, fire mission."

"Send your mission."

The nearest artillery Registration Point was at the southern tip of the nipa grove that hid the NVA. He figured that from the RP they were dug in 150 meters away, a bit east of due north.

"Enemy platoon in a tree line, dug in," he said. "From Omaha, zero-three-zero degrees, add one-five-zero." He almost said "will adjust," but that would get him only a single round to base an adjustment on. He wanted rounds from all five tubes of the battery, and right now. "Fire for effect."

"Roger, wait."

They were re-laying the guns now to fire the mission. He switched back to the command push. "Hello gunship, this is Rover three one."

After the crackle of static, "Weasel two two."

"Be advised, I've got an artillery fire mission in progress." Paxton didn't want the one in a million to happen and have the bird get smacked with a howitzer round.

"Roger, I'm monitoring the FDC push. We've got backup gunships inbound. Should be here in three or four minutes."

"Your last pass was a bit short. I'll mark it with red smoke when you're ready."

"Roger."

"I'm going back to the FDC push now."

"Rover three one, this is Wonder six. What is your current...." Paxton reset the frequency, listening for word that the rounds were on the way.

While he waited, he tore open Sanders' shirt and began tying the bleeding man's battle dressing around the wounded arm. As he worked, he looked around. One paddy dike behind him and a bit to his left, Casey Jones was just lofting an M79 round into the nipa palm. He got a tree burst just a bit in front of where the NVA machine gun was located. *Nice one.* Paxton motioned him to come up to his immediate left. The grenadier rolled himself over the dike, hugging tight against it, then low-crawled across the paddy to Paxton's left, holding his weapon just above the water. They both knew he was scooping a leech or two inside his fatigue shirt in the process. *Now—where the hell is Janowitz?*

As he looked around for Janowitz, he absently rubbed his mouth and nose, then realized the back of his hand had come away with blood on it, the sticky kind that's already half dried. He wondered if the initial explosion ruptured his eardrums, causing blood to seep out of his nostrils. He gingerly tried the airplane-passenger trick for altitude changes, forcing a sort of yawn, but it felt okay. He rubbed at his ear and got half-dried blood again, along with some crusting paddy muck. He decided red and brown must be plastered over most of his face. But he had to be bleeding somewhere. And then his stomach contracted into a sharp knot of pain and he groaned out loud.

Sanders caught the sound. "Sarge, you hit?"

"Kessler," he murmured, staring at his hand.

"Who?" Sanders shouted.

"Kessler," he said louder.

"I haven't seen him," Sanders responded. "You know where he is?"

Paxton wiped his hand on his thigh. "He's Kilo." He spat it out harshly, using the phonetic identifier for the first letter of KIA. Sanders slumped a little, his head inclining slightly forward. His lips moved soundlessly for a second.

"Hey, Sarge." It was Casey Jones. "Where's Janowitz?"

The radio crackled. "Shot, over."

Paxton grabbed the handset. "Shot, out." The artillery rounds were on their way. He looked around. "Janowitz," he shouted, "where are you?"

Casey spotted him. "There!" He pointed back the way they had come. Ken was 50 meters south of their consolidated position.

How the hell did he get stuck back there? "Move up! Move up!" Paxton shouted. He gave the hand signal for 'assemble on me,' circling his right hand overhead, index finger up. He had to get everybody together, to concentrate their fire and be ready to make a dash whenever the slick came back.

Ken got no farther than ten feet in a low, crouching run before automatic fire kicked up the water all around him, making it look like someone was throwing handfuls of gravel into the paddy. He dove back prone where he was, and then the artillery was roaring in. All at once, five enormous umbrellas of dense gray smoke and debris mushroomed up along both sides of the tree line, followed a split second later by the *crump* of the impact and explosion. With a casualty radius of 50 meters for each shell, the range couldn't be better. "Fire for effect!" he yelled into the handset, and got a roger.

"Rover, this is Weasel two two. Can you check out my people in that downed bird?"

Shit! Paxton had already forgotten the gunship lying on its side in the paddy. "Roger."

He looked at the tree line. After the artillery rounds, there were no green tracers. He wasn't inexperienced enough to think that all the bad guys were dead, but at least they were deep in their holes with their ears ringing, and the smoke and swirling earth set in motion by the explosions were obscuring their view of Paxton's position for the moment.

"Cover me," he yelled, and sprang up out of the water and onto the paddy dike, moving at a dead run toward the chopper. The possibility of booby traps on the dike was a calculated risk, nothing he could do about that. As he ran along with his rifle at high port, he realized he hadn't even fired it yet—*crazy war.* In the last few moments of his 15-second sprint, he heard the snap of AK47 rounds right by his ear and glimpsed a green tracer in front of him and high. He angled back into the paddies and threw himself down, rolling completely over from the push of his momentum. When he came to rest and raised his head, he was looking down the barrel of a pistol.

It was the pilot of the gunship. "Are you hit?" Paxton asked.

"Took a round through my right foot," he answered. "Not bleeding bad, but I think the bones are messed up." He was nursing a frizzled strand of leather out of the bloody tangle of his boot and foot. "Same place I took a round my last tour, you believe that? Exact same place."

Paxton believed it. He pulled the field dressing out of his first aid pouch and quickly tied it around the aviator's wounded foot, leaving the gashed boot in place. He started for the bird to get the other aviator.

"Save it," the other said curtly. "He's bought it."

Paxton's mouth went taut for a moment. Then he said, "Okay, let's get you back by the radio." As he bent to get a grip on the pilot, a rocket-propelled grenade struck the downed helicopter amidships, blasting fragments and bits of wreckage in every direction. A chunk of gunship slammed into the back of Paxton's left arm two inches above the elbow, spun him halfway around, and dropped him on his back in the paddy.

The pilot rolled and squirmed himself over to Paxton. "Where are you hit?"

"Left arm."

"Try to wiggle your fingers." They moved okay. The aviator took pieces of lace out of the remains of the boot on his wounded foot and began tying them together. "You're bleeding kind of heavy. I'm going to put a tourniquet on." He pushed the torn left sleeve up and tied the lace around the arm above the wound. Paxton started to put his right arm around him to move him, but the pilot said, "Wait." He stuck his thumb into the ooze of Paxton's wound and used it to paint a T on his forehead, so if Paxton passed out later any medics would know to look for a tourniquet. *Ash Wednesday,* Paxton thought, and allowed himself a brief ironic smile.

He dragged the aviator through the water to a dike that marked the halfway point back to Sanders and the radio, and fell heavily against it. "I hate these paddies," Paxton said, panting. He wrestled the airman 90 degrees around, so that he was parallel to the dike and right up against it. "They're not only full of leeches, but the farmers all take their dumps in 'em. They think the shit makes the rice grow better." He pushed the airman partway up the dike and then laid his shoulder against his back, heaving him up and over by main force into the next paddy. He followed right after him and landed

25

squarely on top of the pilot, pushing his head underwater before he rolled beyond him. The aviator came up coughing and spitting.

"I wish you hadn't told me the recipe for this stuff," he said, blowing water out of his nose.

Getting the pilot to the radio took two more slow-motion rushes. His left hand could grasp okay, but it was no good for heavy lifting. The last 15 feet the AK47s found the range and kicked up the water all around them until the next artillery rounds pushed them back down in their holes. Paxton had just enough time to get the aviator to the radio before the NVA machine gun started up again. They'd figured out how much time they had between salvos.

"Weasel, this is Rover three one. I've got one of your people here, wounded. The other one didn't make it."

"Roger. Who've you got?"

"Tell him Baker." Paxton did.

"Roger. Be advised, we've got two more gunships arriving on station now and we're going to try the extraction again. I'm lifting the artillery fire. Your slick is inbound, about a minute out. Put red smoke on the enemy location and mark your position again for the slick."

"Roger," he said into the handset. He turned to Casey Jones. "Casey! Put red smoke on that machine gun." As the grenadier started to replace the high explosive round in his M79, Paxton tossed a smoke grenade into the water. The NVA greeted the yellow cloud bubbling up with an increasing intensity of fire.

Oh shit! "Janowitz! Janowitz, get up here on the double!" He tried to raise himself, looking where he'd last seen him, but the incoming small arms fire was too intense.

"Sarge, they got him." It was Al Gomez. "While you were at the gunship, I yelled at him to get over here with us. He rose up to make a run for it, and an RPG round went off right under his feet."

First Kessler, now Janowitz. Send your best squad leader...

"Rover, where's that red smoke? We need to start our run."

"Casey, get that red smoke on their machine gun!"

The grenadier lay up against the paddy dike, holding his grenade launcher atop it as he waited for a lessening in the fire brought on by the yellow smoke. He steeled himself, then knelt upright on his right knee in the paddy water, bracing his left foot against the dike. He took quick aim and got off the shot as three machine gun rounds struck him in the chest, hitting with the force of sharp punches. His arms flew up, the grenade launcher looping away, and he sprawled out flat on his back in the paddy water. His smoke round landed right on target, marking the enemy machine gun with red.

Why'd he raise up so high? Paxton ran over to him, knowing before he got there that he was dead.

"Sarge!" Gomez yelled. Paxton looked up from the grenadier's body to see the slick, inbound 50 meters south, its starboard door gunner pouring a continuous stream of orange tracers into the NVA position. At the same time, the three gunships were just beginning their firing pass in trail, one behind the other. They timed the run for the crucial few seconds when the pilot of the slick had to hold his helicopter in a tight hover a foot above the water, the perfect target. Paxton and Gomez loaded the wounded aviator into the slick with the help of the port door gunner. Schiller was holding just short of the tail rotor, running his last belt of ammo through the M60, shooting with fair accuracy considering he was firing from the hip. Finally, the wounded Sanders went in.

"Schiller! Now!" Paxton shouted, wondering if he'd hear him above the full-revving roar of the slick. But Schiller ceased fire and ran to the port door of the copter, jumping up onto the runner and springing into the bird right after Gomez and Paxton. The door gunner spoke into his headset and the slick lurched sharply forward. Gathering speed, it banked hard left, away from the NVA tree line. In a quick look back, Paxton caught a view, like a snapshot, of the downed gunship close to Kessler's body. It was curled in on itself, not far from Casey Jones, who lay spread-eagled in the middle of the paddy. Janowitz would be half a football field away to the southwest, his body badly cut up by the shrapnel from the RPG round. *Why didn't he keep up with the rest of us?* The feelings that always took control of him after a firefight were already creeping in, making him question his decisions and actions. And now with the adrenaline petering out, the wound in his left arm was radiating with pain.

"Nice going."

He looked up at the aviator, not comprehending. Paxton could tell from his face that he was in pain from the wound in his foot. The pilot leaned closer to his ear. "You did a hell of a job back there."

Paxton gave a mechanical half smile to indicate that he'd heard. Some job. Walked smack into the middle of an ambush, got a gunship shot down, took four KIA and three WIA, including the helicopter guys. With the wound in his arm throbbing the way it was, why did he feel so numb?

The door gunner leaned down to them. "We're going into Third Field Hospital at Tan Son Nhut," he told them. The aviator's face was very pale.

"How long?" Paxton asked.

"ETA is one zero," the door gunner answered.

The aviator looked relieved. "Well anyway, that's good news."

The door gunner shook his head. "There's fighting all over the delta right now. Third Field's in mass casualty mode."

CHAPTER 2

Two medics eased the aviator onto a stretcher and carried him, ashen now from loss of blood and intensifying pain, past the waiting wounded into triage. The tone of Mingo Sanders' dark brown skin took on a washed-out look on the flight, and Paxton decided he must have lost more blood from his shoulder than it looked like. Concerned, Gomez supported Sanders and walked him slowly into triage behind the stretcher. Only Paxton and Ted Schiller walked in by themselves.

Carmen Griggs looked over at them. She wore captain's bars on her right collar and the caduceus of an army nurse on her left. She stood beside a patient whose thorax was laid open, exposing part of his left lung. Across from her, Dr. Harold Rasmussen was just realizing that in addition to the massive chest wound, the patient's spine had been virtually severed by a piece of shrapnel. He could just see the tip protruding from the wound.

"Expectant," he said to the medics, and they moved the soldier to one side with two others. Their treatment would consist of being made as comfortable as possible in what little time they had left. None of them was conscious.

Rasmussen stepped around a man with a deep, jagged wound in his left thigh and began examining Baker's foot. Carmen Griggs went to Sanders, who looked on the point of keeling over.

"Pretty torn up," Baker said to the doctor.

"Got that right." Rasmussen gingerly lifted a corner of the battle dressing and looked at the mess under it. A round had struck the aviator's foot at the base of the heel and tumbled its way through the metatarsals, exiting at the middle toe after ripping muscles and bones beyond any hope of reconstruction. He thought of the German word for hamburger—hackfleisch, chopped meat. It would have to come off.

"Can you save it?"

Rasmussen smiled at the aviator. "Give it our best shot." To the medics he said, "Hang Ringer's lactate with ten milligrams of morphine. Immediate." In seconds they were rigging the IV.

As Griggs was looking at the wounded right arm of Sanders, his left hand groped vaguely toward his throat and his legs began to buckle. Paxton realized Sanders was gasping for air but not getting any, and the sound of his gagging along with his body's struggles was eerie. In a moment, his eyes rolled back and he lost consciousness. The nurse inserted an oral airway down Sanders' mouth, but his struggle to breathe continued. As she called out "Doctor," the femoral artery ruptured on the patient with the thigh wound and began to hemorrhage. Rasmussen snatched up a fresh battle dressing from the pile they kept handy and controlled the flow with pressure.

"Doctor," Griggs called again. "Deviated airway here. I think shrapnel's nicked the carotid. Tracheotomy, stat."

"You do it, Red. I've got to patch this guy's femoral, and right now."

He called her Red.

The medics moved from Baker's stretcher and picked up the man with the thigh wound. Rasmussen headed toward surgery, still pressing against the hemorrhaging artery. On the move, he said to Baker, "We'll get you as soon as we can. The morphine will keep the pain down." And he was gone.

Griggs knelt down by Sanders as a medic laid a packet of instruments wrapped in green cloth on his chest. Another helicopter was setting down on the pad outside and the medic, stating the obvious, said, "Inbound."

She motioned him with her head to go to it. As he hurried out, she flipped open the sterile green material, picked up a scalpel and poised it above Sanders' throat. She hesitated and looked around. Gomez stood directly across from her. She grabbed his sleeve and pulled him down beside her.

"Hold this by his throat," she said, and thrust a battle dressing into his hand. "Here. No, right here. That's it. Good." Then she made the incision. At once, blood spattered out under pressure, much of it caught by the dressing Gomez held. As Sanders began to breathe again, more blood coughed out. When the flow abated, she inserted a flexible tube connected to a bottle and suctioned blood and mucus from his airway. She was checking his blood pressure when his eyes fluttered open. She had obviously done this before.

She looked toward the helipad entrance as two more wounded, both on stretchers, were brought into triage. She stood to go to them, but other staff moved in quickly and began checking them out. Her eyes fell on Paxton.

"Where's the tourniquet?" she asked.

"What? Oh, left arm."

Taking a pair of medical scissors out of her pocket, she cut straight up his sleeve past the tourniquet, on across the shoulder and through the collar. She took the M16 out of his right hand, pulled the shirt down his right arm, and threw the remnants on a pile of slashed uniform pieces and bloody medical waste.

She held the weapon up. It was still locked and loaded. "Big no-no," she said.

She depressed the detent, freeing the magazine in its well, and pulled it out. Then with a swift downward motion of her right hand, she cleared the last round from the chamber.

Schiller retrieved the bullet from the floor and took the magazine from her. She looked at him and his machine gun. "You too, handsome."

For an instant, Schiller was blank, and then he followed her gaze to his weapon. He flipped up the cover and removed a three-inch length of linked ammo. As he held it up for Paxton to see, his eyes widened.

"Seven rounds left," Schiller said to Paxton.

"Near thing."

A GI on the hospital staff collected and tagged their weapons after telling them where to reclaim them.

Visibly pale, Schiller was realizing how close he had come to being left with nothing but his .45-caliber pistol. "I need a cigarette," he muttered, and headed for the nearest door.

"That's surgery," Griggs said. "Over there." She nodded toward another entry. Long ago Paxton figured out that the only time Schiller was really sure of himself and knew what to do was in a firefight. Somewhere inside was a little boy, and right now the kid was plainly shaken. Paxton motioned for Al Gomez to follow Schiller and keep an eye on him.

The nurse turned back to Paxton, hands on hips, and frankly appraised his torso. "Jock?" she asked.

Round eye alert. "Yeah."

She moved in to him, checked his arm and laid her hand easily on his chest. "What sport?" Her fingers glided over him, as if searching for some wound or abrasion. Paxton felt himself tensing, and his penis began a purposeful stirring. "Track. And some baseball."

She smiled at him. "In pain?"

His arm hurt, but it would keep. Sexually, he was ready to deal. But at the same time, around the edges of his consciousness, shadows were trying to separate themselves from the deeper blackness they now dwelt in. The Old Man and the entire company would already be on the ground at LZ Cody. They'd get a body count, and police up enemy weapons and documents. And they'd gather in Matt Kessler, Casey Jones and Ken Janowitz, the shadows lurking at the verges of his mind, and get them on their way to Graves Registration. Well before dark, a Sky Crane would fly in to recover the downed gunship and then the company would be able to recommence its move back to base camp. By the time the sun sank below the horizon, the expanse of paddy would look the way it had yesterday, or last week, or a hundred years ago.

"Yeah, it kind of hurts." He found that his erection had begun to subside, while her face was in the process of clouding over in light of his oblique 'no thanks.'

She seized his tourniquet more roughly than necessary, and he winced. "Who the hell tied this on?" When she cut it, there was no unusual bleeding.

"Baker," he answered, and nodded toward the wounded aviator on the floor.

She looked down at him. He was resting on his elbow watching their gambit. His face was pale and sweat misted his forehead, but he wore a big grin.

"I'm a jock, too. Wrestling," Baker said, eyeing the nurse. "Want to wrestle?" He cocked his head sideways and waggled his eyebrows. Griggs laughed, despite herself.

"Oh, you wild beast, you." She checked the drip on his IV and then caught sight of a widening spot of blood on the sleeve of his other arm. She knelt beside him and pulled the zipper at his throat down to his middle. "I love these aviator jump suits. One zip at the neck and another at the crotch, but they're both on the same zipper." She pushed the uniform aside to expose his shoulder and upper arm. "With a rig like this, you can't tell whether you're coming or going."

"Oh, I know when I'm coming, Captain," he said, his grin widening. "Hey, that stuff the doc put in my transfusion is real kicky. Why don't you throw in another jigger?"

Paxton held the uniform back, while she swabbed a small cut on the aviator's arm. "Way too soon for another one of those," she replied. "Don't worry. We'll keep you in never-never land for a while."

When the two medics returned to take him into surgery, he gave them a big grin. "Hi, guys." As they carried him out, she stood and turned to Paxton. "Now for you, young strapping jock."

As she began examining the wound again, he clenched his teeth, but she was more gentle, more professional. He was relieved.

"Do you know what got you?" She began preparing a hypodermic.

"A piece of helicopter, I think, when an RPG round hit it."

"Well," she said, swabbing his arm, "I've got good news and bad news. The good news, no significant damage. An inch this way and you could have had big-time problems with muscles and nerves in your arm, and three or four inches over here and you'd have probably gotten your lung perforated."

"You mean like a sucking chest wound?" He'd seen a few of those. The punctured lung would collapse and then just the simple act of breathing got tricky.

"Exactly." She began working her way around his wound with the hypodermic, emptying a bit of its contents at each location.

"Am I going to never-never land?"

"No. This is just a local, lidocaine with epinephrine. You're only going to need half a dozen stitches or so." She set the syringe aside and prepared to scrub out the wound with betadine. "Looks like whatever it was hit and glanced off."

He watched her preparations. "Shouldn't a doctor do this?"

"Yes, well..." She smiled and began to scrub the wound vigorously with a brush. "Sometimes, we have to cross-level the workload." She was going at it with a will, making a dark red foam out of the betadine and blood. He could feel the vigorous back-and-forth of the brush, but there was no real pain. She sponged the area and then began to suture his wound.

"What's the bad news?"

"After a few days of light duty, you're going back out there."

He laughed, which brought a surprised expression to her face. But he was thinking of his squad, or rather the remnants of it. Although he was authorized eleven men, only Gomez, Schiller and himself would be ready for duty. Third squad: combat ineffective.

She glanced up at his face a second. "I don't usually get turned down," she said. He laughed again, through an ironic smile, which again was not what she expected. It angered her. "You *are* standard male persuasion, aren't you?" she asked sarcastically.

"Look, Captain." Maybe using her rank would jog her out of this grab-ass attitude of hers. "I just lost over half my squad killed and wounded. This may surprise you, but the most important thing on my mind right now is not a shot of P." He had almost said 'sex,' but that was way too neutral for what he wanted to convey. 'A shot of P' was the current brevity code for pussy. She colored and he fully expected her to find a non-anesthetized spot or two, but she continued her suturing with apparent equanimity. After a moment, he said, "Sorry."

She shrugged with her eyebrows, while her hands went on working. "Point well taken." She paused a second, and her face grew frank. "Some of the hospital people get through all this with booze. Some self-medicate." She looked him in the eye. "Me, I get physical." She began tying off.

"Booze, dick, pills—fine. But hang with your own people, will you? Don't slop it over on us when we're like this." His head gesture took in the whole room, then his anger diluted to frustrated complaint. "Why am I telling *you* this? You should be telling *me*."

She simply smiled as she finished and then went to the drug cabinet. "Take one of these every four hours for pain, as needed. No closer together than that. They'll mess with your mind."

"Never-never land?"

"Yeah, place of the weird geography. I'm only giving you four of these. But if you don't need them, don't take them."

The round white pills were just a bit larger than aspirin. He put one in his mouth and reached for his canteen.

"You can use the drinking fountain over there." They smiled at each other over that. The clock above the fountain read 1545 hours. As he put the bottle of pills in his pocket and bent to drink, Schiller returned.

"Glad you're back," she said to him. "Come on, I want to check you out."

Paxton already felt the exhausting tension flowing out of his body and sensed a re-energizing taking place. *Is the medication that fast?* She led Schiller back toward the door he'd just come through. Clarity flooded over Paxton, pushing the shadow figures of Kessler and Casey Jones and Ken Janowitz back beyond his mind's horizon. He felt anger giving way to cunning, revulsion at her aggressiveness changing to an aggressiveness of his own.

"What was your sport?" she asked Schiller. "Basketball?"

Could the pill be working on his mind already? Or knowing that it soon would, had that become a permission for his mind to work on itself? Her defiant eyes caught Paxton's for a split second, then she and Schiller went out the door.

A sly smile played across his face. He knew what she was up to. The edges of his vision seemed filtered through water and brighter somehow than the middle—even sparkling. He wouldn't let her get away with marauding poor little Schiller. He looked instinctively for his rifle, then remembered it waited for him in the hospital arms room. He followed them through the door, but they were nowhere to be seen.

He strode easily down the hall. Although he was stripped to the waist and still wore his pistol belt and canteen, none of the hospital staff took the slightest notice of him. Each ceiling light glowed with its own power, surrounded by a halo of luminescence that was sharp and clear on its inside edge, blurry but bright on the outside. He passed a door on the left marked *Staff Only*. On the right, a sign stenciled with an arrow and *Surgery* pointed down a side hall. He continued straight ahead, past another door on the left that read *Off Limits,* and halted when his corridor came to a T with another. The left side went out of the building. Through the doorway, he could see GIs smoking. The way right led straight ahead to the administrative part of the hospital, with a branch hallway 30 feet down, *To Snack Bar.*

He turned and looked back the way he'd come, certain that the translucence of his vision brought on by the medication would reveal them to him. Then the off-limits door swung open and Schiller's panicky momentum carried him into the middle of the empty hallway. His right hand gripped his helmet while his left held up his pants, which were unzipped and gaping open. Paxton went to him and took the helmet from him.

"Do yourself up," he said.

Schiller's eyes were pleading. "She wanted to...."

"I know. Do yourself up." He did and Paxton gave him back his headgear. "Is she still in there? Is this the only way out?"

Before Schiller could answer, the door swung open again. When Griggs saw Paxton, she stopped and leaned against the doorway. Schiller moved to put Paxton between him and the nurse. He actually looked frightened.

Paxton's eyes were glowing. He could feel it and he was sure Griggs could see it. "Go find Gomez," he told Schiller, "and wait for me in the snack bar. I've got business." His smile declared complete control. Schiller went.

"Well, Jock…"

Still smiling, he said, "Shut up." He took her firmly by the upper arm and turned her back into the room. He didn't feel so much light-headed as floating, not so much disconnected as free. What was in those pills? The mechanical pull clicked the door shut and he checked the knob for a locking device.

"It locks automatically."

"I'll bet." He looked around the room. It had been a one-seater bathroom about six by ten, much too roomy by military standards, which had been turned into a supply room. One of the long walls held the commode, a utility sink, and a small cabinet, probably for toilet-cleaning materials. Wall-to-wall open shelving stood opposite, stocked with various medical supplies. At the foot of the short wall facing the door lay an inflated air mattress.

"Fixed up a nice on-your-back shack," he said.

"What makes you think the offer's still good?" He could tell from her eyes that she expected him to follow her script.

"Oh, man," he said, and shook his head. "You're pathetic, you know that?"

"What?" Doubt began edging into her eyes. "What are you talking about?"

"Are you people in mass casualty mode here or not? Another helicopter just set down out there, and here you are, shopping for a quick one with Schiller."

"Is that his name? A very limp specimen."

She was trying to brazen it out, but Paxton wouldn't let her. "What the hell kind of a nurse are you, anyway?"

"Don't you talk to me like that, Sergeant." The words should have been an attack, but to Paxton's ear they seemed completely defensive.

"If you'd pulled somebody in here five minutes earlier, *Captain*," he said, emphasizing her rank with sarcasm, "there'd have been nobody out there to open up Sanders' throat. He'd be dead right now."

For a moment, she seemed at a loss. Then she said, "I have never once, not in my whole career..."

He cut her off. "Oh, stop it. If you wouldn't drink on duty, you shouldn't be doing this."

"Listen, if you're not man enough to..."

At that moment, the door to the room burst open and an army nurse with the eagles of a full Colonel strode in, holding a clutch of keys. She looked from Paxton, stripped to the waist, to the air mattress against the wall. She was livid.

"Well, Griggs," the Colonel said to Red. "Strike two."

"Colonel Martin, I...."

"I told you once—I don't care what you do on your own time, as long as it's not in my hospital."

"Ma'am," Paxton interjected.

"Shut up." She didn't even look at him. "If I ever find you like this again, Captain Griggs—in any location while you're on duty, or at any time within the confines of my hospital—I will not only court-martial you out of the Army. I will cheerfully inform the state of Oregon, which was foolish enough to license you, that you are unfit to be a member of the nursing profession."

"Ma'am, Captain Griggs brought me in here to find me some extra bandages for my wound." Paxton waved vaguely at the shelves of medical supplies.

She finally looked at the half-naked Paxton. "If you ever

come in my hospital again," she said, "you'd better be on a stretcher or I'll put you on one. Now get out."

He believed her, but for some reason he didn't want to leave Red dangling if he could help it. "Ma'am..."

"Get out!" She was barely containing her anger. "I've got a few more choice words that only Griggs should hear."

He tried once more. "But, Ma'am..."

"Get! Out!"

He got, heading for the snack bar.

※

The irony of the Colonel mistaking why he was in the room wasn't lost on him, but it didn't make a bit of difference. She'd taken off a layer of his skin just in passing. Right now, she was probably disassembling Red piece by piece.

He wondered why he'd tried to get her off the hook with her boss. When he thought about it, he couldn't get past those green eyes of hers. Some part of how she felt about that room and its doings had seeped into them, had tensed the beginnings of crow's feet at their corners. She didn't like what she did in that room but understood why she had to go there, and to an extent accepted that in herself. Paxton realized then that a person didn't have to be in battle out in the field to be harmed by its aftermath. And as he recognized what was happening in her, he knew that something like it had happened in himself. He realized he had fallen from the easy heights of Hollywood war heroes and the solemn rites of Memorial Day, down to the here-and-now reality of Charles Paxton, squad leader: four men killed today, three wounded.

A dumpling of a Red Cross lady interrupted his thoughts by taking him in hand and not releasing him until his face was clean, he wore a fresh fatigue shirt, and he took a glass of her orange juice. Once around the corner, he got rid of the drink and tore the left sleeve off at the shoulder, so it wouldn't rub against his wound.

When he reached the snack bar, he got a 20-ounce cup of Coke, poured over a pile of ice that went clear up to the brim, and sat down with Schiller and Gomez. When he took his first long pull, the sugar and caffeine gave a nice little jolt and the carbonation made his eyes water. But it was the ice, the *ice,* that he really wanted. He wrapped both hands around the cup, taking genuine pleasure from the rattle when he shook it. He relished the cold wetness gathering on its outside and the feel as he crunched on a cube.

Alive.

"What was with that nurse?" Schiller asked.

"She's hooked on dick."

Gomez immediately alerted. "Who? That round eye in triage?"

"Yeah," Schiller responded. "She took me in that room and had my pants open in 30 seconds."

Gomez looked like he wanted to believe it but knew Schiller too well. "Come on, man, don't shit me now."

"It's true," Paxton confirmed.

Gomez looked at Schiller incredulously. "You got some of that?"

"No." His eyes wavered. "After that firefight today, I couldn't get it up."

"I know," Paxton said. "I turned her down, too." Schiller looked relieved. "Even after she gave me some pills," he added.

Gomez became very focused. "Pills to get it up?"

Paxton laughed. "No, to kill the pain," he said, shrugging his wounded left arm at him. "But they also…" He fluttered his fingers next to his head. "You know?"

"Sarge, the truth now," Gomez demanded. His eyes narrowed. "Did you nail that lady?"

Paxton shook his head. "No." He paused, then shrugged. "I couldn't stop thinking about Kessler and the guys." They sat in silence for maybe ten seconds, then Paxton roused himself. He told Gomez about the air mattress, which Schiller confirmed. Then he went into the story of the Colonel walking in and finding Paxton standing there half naked, and they all laughed.

"Son of a *gun,* Sarge. You got the touch."

"All we did was shake hands."

"Yeah, but a round eye." Gomez always made sure he got his rocks off at Mama Huong's when they came back from the field, but he hadn't been with an American woman since he got in country. He was clearly jealous.

Paxton knew the story would be all over the company by this time tomorrow, and he didn't mind that at all. He grinned.

Another pill in three more hours....

Out of the corner of his eye, he recognized the GI just sitting down at the next table. It was the medic who handed Red the packet of instruments when she opened Mingo Sanders' throat. The dark gray holes his eyes sat in looked just like Red's. He had two large drink cups on his tray, two cans of beer and two small containers of tomato juice. *Is he meeting someone or is that all for him?* He popped one of the beers and tilted the cup to keep the foam down as he poured. Then he pulled the tab off a tomato juice and poured it in on top of the beer. He repeated the process a second time and, while the mix in the two cups cured, he lit a cigarette.

Judging from his face, he didn't get much sleep—at least not good sleep. Paxton noticed the small burn holes in his fatigue shirt where the live tips of past cigarettes had fallen unnoticed. How could that happen? Where's his head when the lit end drops and sticks? He looked at the face again. Wherever his head liked to go, it was there now. He sat with elbows on the table, right hand curled around left in front of his face, holding a cigarette that already had a dangerously long tip. *Time to get out of here.*

He finished his Coke and told them to try and scrounge up a ride back to base camp. A chopper would be nice, although not likely, and would save them at least an hour on the road. While they did that, he'd find a phone and check in with the First Sergeant.

He decided the infantry god must have heard his prayer because he didn't meet the Colonel of nurses on the way to the admin section of the hospital. At the info desk across from the main entrance, a PFC let him use the phone. After a few minutes, he got patched through to Bearcat main switch and then to the orderly room. "Top, it's Paxton."

"How are you?" He sounded worried.

"Some stitches in my left arm. I was lucky."

"Another Purple Heart."

"Yeah."

"You don't need any more, you know."

"Tell me."

"How about the rest?"

"Gomez and Schiller are okay. They had to do a tracheotomy on Sanders, but he should make it. The chopper pilot's foot doesn't look good."

"Sounds like a hell of a firefight."

"It was real squeaky till I got the artillery cranked up. Schiller had seven rounds left."

"Jesus." Top paused. "Are you going to have to overnight there?" He had something on his mind.

"I've got Gomez and Schiller hunting up a ride. If we can hit the road soon, we'll close in to Bearcat before dark."

"Paxton, listen now. I need you to do something."

Paxton tensed. He'd used that exact wording and tone of voice the time he ran out of soldiers on company punishment. He'd told Paxton that his squad had to pull the honey buckets from under the shitters and burn them out with diesel fuel.

"First Sergeant, what are you going to put on me?"

"I need you to go over to the Tan Son Nhut mortuary and ID your people."

43

Paxton couldn't believe what he was hearing. "Goddam it, Top."

"It won't take you a minute. It's just Kessler and Casey Jones."

"And Janowitz."

"They never found Janowitz."

"What?"

"I mean they never found him."

An image flashed into his mind of Janowitz floating face down in the water, alone in the middle of a vast stretch of deserted paddies. "He was no more than 50 meters south. He's got to be there."

"Well, as of right now he's MIA, so you've only got two IDs to make."

"I'm not going to do this, Top."

"Simmer down, Paxton."

"You're the enlisted honch in the company, not me."

"Look. They usually bring the bodies into Graves Registration here at Bearcat where I can get to them, but they didn't this time."

"Where are they?"

"The bird was getting low on fuel, so they flew them straight to Tan Son Nhut to the field hospital."

"You mean they're *here?*" Paxton suddenly felt like the place was shrinking in on him.

"They move them by vehicle from there over to the mortuary."

"Top, I don't want to do this."

"It would cost me most of a day to get up there and back. Just do the ID and forget it." His voice hardened. "You're in their chain of command same as me, Paxton, and you're right there on the ground with them. Now you get over to that mortuary and do your job." He paused, easing back a bit. "When you're done, go find a bed at the BEQ, and then get good and wasted at the NCO club."

44

Paxton groped in silence for other options for so long that the First Sergeant must have thought their connection had been broken. "Hello? Paxton?"

He felt boxed in with no way out. "Don't do this to me, Top." He tried not to sound like he was begging.

"Don't do what?" The outrage in the First Sergeant's voice confirmed for Paxton that Top was riding a guilt trip for pinning this on him and was covering it with an attitude. "This comes with your stripes, Sergeant. Now get over there and do it." He broke their connection.

He didn't think he could force himself to look at Kessler again the way he was now. It was that simple. That's what pulled on him. But then he realized he couldn't leave Kessler abandoned either—unclaimed, unacknowledged, officially nameless until Paxton gave him one. That began pulling him in the opposite direction.

The PFC at the info desk spoke up. "Is your First making you do an ID?"

"Yeah." Paxton attempted a little smile. "I was standing right next to him when he got hit."

"Wimmer's about to make a run over there. He can give you a ride." As he picked up the phone, Gomez and Schiller came up.

"We found a five-ton heading back to Bearcat," Gomez said. "They're waiting for us."

"The driver said he likes riding with infantry in the back of the truck." Schiller grinned. "I didn't tell him I'm down to seven rounds."

Gomez looked at Paxton. "What's wrong?"

Paxton shrugged. "Top wants me to ID Kessler and Casey Jones."

"Son of a *gun*, Sarge." Gomez shook his head. "He shouldn't make you do that."

"That's not all. Janowitz is missing."

"What?"

45

"That's what he said."

Gomez was incredulous. "I saw the whole thing. The RPG round hit him and knocked him up in the air and then he fell back into the paddy. He should have been right there."

"It's broad daylight out there," Schiller said. "They should have spotted him from the helicopters going in."

A thought struck Gomez. "You don't think dogs got him, do you? Dragged him off?"

"I don't know," Paxton answered.

When farmers abandoned the land, they sometimes ate their dogs, and sometimes the animals simply ran off when the fighting got close. Then they turned wild and banded together into packs to hunt. Paxton was sure all three of them were thinking about the time the squad surprised a pack at the body of an NVA soldier in a dense grove of nipa. He'd been dead several days and before they actually saw him, they caught the stink of his body hanging on the humid air. They heard the dogs working at him, the occasional snap and yip of disagreement and the slavering growls. Paxton didn't know when he picked up the knowledge, but he knew from the smell that it was an NVA soldier and not an ox or a goat—or a GI. In death, each species seemed to have its own distinct odor and he'd gained the ability to distinguish among them, a job skill probably only a soldier ever acquired.

Once they could see the half-dozen feeding animals, they killed them all. It didn't matter to the dogs which uniform it was. An unburied soldier was meat—it could just as well have been a GI. Right now, it could be Janowitz. His men had stood quietly while Paxton defied the stench to scatter a handful of wet earth on the NVA soldier's body. Later, after the third firefight in a row where he'd lost people, Paxton knew he'd never be strewing dirt on an enemy again.

"Who needs the ride to the mortuary?" It was the medic with the cigarette burns in his shirt, standing in the main door.

"Here's Wimmer, Sergeant," the PFC behind the desk said. "He'll give you a lift."

"You guys head back to Bearcat," Paxton told them, as they retrieved their weapons from the arms room. "Tell Top I'll see him when I see him."

Paxton and Wimmer slid into the front of a canvas-covered five-ton truck and the medic moved them out into traffic. Neither spoke. In some ways, it was like any army post back home, except that the jeep going by in the opposite direction had live ammo locked and loaded in its pedestal-mounted machine gun. When they passed an MP giving a driver a speeding ticket, Paxton could only smile and shake his head. They moved into a tent city, the sides rolled up for the scant breeze. Traffic thinned out a bit.

"Much farther?" Paxton asked.

"Three or four minutes."

"Make the run often?"

"As needed."

Paxton wondered what 'as needed' meant, and then as the implication hit him he froze. "What's in the back?"

"KIAs." His voice was matter of fact, almost dulled out. *Is Kessler back there?*

"Any flown in from the field?"

"Yeah, three came straight in, plus three expectants, and two others I picked up earlier."

Three, straight into the hospital. *He is, he's back there. The chopper pilot, Casey Jones and Kessler.* He was feeling the same stabbing pain in his belly that he'd gotten when he realized Kessler's blood was smeared across his face. He tried to stay calm. "What are expectants?" High cirrus clouds began subtly dimming back the sun.

"Wounded that come into triage and aren't expected to live—and don't."

He began thinking about the dead NVA again, violated by the dogs. He tried to shake the scene, but it only grew more vivid, to the point where the old oppressive smell started insidiously to infiltrate into his consciousness. The visual image was so potent, it brought the odor in its wake. Paxton actually hawked a couple of times to clear the smell-taste out of his nostrils and throat. He spat out the window and then noticed a few fine specks of gray gathering on the windshield. Wimmer hit the wiper button once to clear the glass.

"What's that stuff?" Paxton asked.

"Ashes," Wimmer answered. "When they get the bodies over there, they cut the uniforms off them. When they get a good pile, which is pretty often, they burn them. You get this ashy stuff then, drifting around. And the smell—it's already in the cloth and it spreads with the soot."

Paxton was stunned. The smell was real, not some figment. And it wasn't any high cloud cover that was dissipating the light. He began to look forward to getting back out to the field.

"And that's not the worst of it," Wimmer continued. "You came in with that pilot, didn't you? The one who took a round in the foot?"

Paxton nodded numbly.

"Well, that's back there, too. They had to take it off. And that goes in the furnace along with the choice body parts of other lucky troops."

Wimmer's sarcastic words sickened Paxton, but he understood that it was a survival mechanism. "I'll tell you what," he said fervently to the medic. "If I had to do this, I'd go crazy."

"Think so?" Wimmer looked at him, gauging how much of this Paxton could tolerate. "I sleep right over there." He nodded in the direction of the tents they were driving past, each with a dozen or more folding canvas cots. "Some mornings, I have to wade through this stuff on the way to the mess hall. And then I wonder who I'm walking on to get to my eggs and bacon." He pulled into a driveway and followed it around to the rear of a long one-story building. "I live downwind from Auschwitz, you know?"

Behind the building, a blacktop pad extended out from a loading dock, with the whole area screened at a little distance by opaque plastic sheeting lashed to a cyclone fence. *So neighbors on their way to breakfast don't have to watch bodies being unloaded.* Paxton's stomach fluttered uncomfortably.

And then as Wimmer maneuvered the truck, Paxton saw the loading dock doors roll up like so many garage doors. When gurneys began to come through and Paxton looked at the faces of the Vietnamese civilians pushing them, the sharp, insistent pain again racked his stomach. *How long do I have to stay here?*

Chapter 3

The oriental faces of the workers made him distinctly uneasy. He didn't want them touching the soldiers' corpses. He wondered which of them was taking a body count to pass to the NVA. Behind the gurneys, he could see half a dozen GIs coming and going at various tasks.

He and Wimmer left the truck cab and mounted the loading dock. The Vietnamese dropped the tailgate of the truck and tied back the canvas. All of the remains were in body bags and lying on stretchers. *Which one is Kessler?* As they began moving them to the gurneys, a slender man wearing a white lab coat over an open-collar shirt and civilian slacks approached them. A good six inches shorter than Paxton, he wore dark horn-rimmed glasses and carried a clipboard.

"Mister Ferko, this sergeant's here for an identification."

"George Ferko," he said, reaching out to Paxton.

"Chuck Paxton." He shifted his M16, and they shook hands. Under the circumstances, he considered the handshake a bit formal.

"Oh, Steve, by the way," Ferko said to Wimmer. He was earnest and quite soft-spoken. "We've got some stretchers and body bags out on the hardstand that should be dry by now. You can do a backhaul with them instead of going back empty." He seemed happy about preventing the truck from returning with no cargo.

"Okay," Wimmer said. "And I brought some amputations, too."

Ferko's eyes refocused on a vacant piece of space in the middle distance. "To be treated as unassociable anatomical remains. They shall be incinerated and disposed of locally." Wimmer's eyes flicked over to Paxton for a split second.

"Good," Ferko said, looking back at the medic. "We'll take care of it." He turned to Paxton. "The remains you want to identify. Do you know when they came in?"

"I think they were in the truck with us."

"The ones from the heliport?" Wimmer asked.

"No, from the hospital. Not the expectants, the others."

Wimmer looked at the eight gurneys and their burdens. "Those three there, I think, Mister Ferko."

"Very good." As Wimmer went back to his truck to go and pick up the equipment, Ferko led Paxton to the first of the three gurneys, unzipped the bag without hesitation and pushed the flaps aside.

Paxton had never seen him before. He wore an aviator's uniform like Baker's. His mouth hung slightly open and his eyes were rolled up in his head, so that just an edge of blue showed below the lids. He couldn't see a wound. It struck him that this stranger died while killing the NVA who were trying to kill Paxton's men.

"I don't know him."

Ferko closed the aviator's eyes with a gentle movement and then slowly slid his hand down across his cheek to his throat. "Still warm," he murmured quietly, "still warm. Climate does that." He shook his head. "Climate," he repeated softly, as if naming something unfortunate or inevitable, and infinitely sad. He closed the bag.

The next contained Casey Jones. His eyes showed only white against the dark brown skin. The blood from the bullet wounds had overlapped so that there was a single large stain shaped like a crude three-leaf clover across his fatigue shirt. It was beginning to crust at the edges but was still quite damp in the middle, and actually wet at the small rips in the material.

Get red smoke on that machine gun.

He'd done that. Carrying out Paxton's order, he'd put red smoke on the gun at the cost of his life.

"It's Casey Jones."

"Ah," Ferko said. He laid his clipboard on the gurney next to the body bag, pulled a form out from the sheaf of papers, and slid it to the top of the pile. "Could you fill this out for me?" As he handed him a pen, Paxton read it over:

The remains which I have ____personally viewed ____seen photographs of (check one) are those of

NAME   GRADE   SERVICE #   ORGANIZATION

I recognize the remains because of the following: (facial features, scars, birthmarks, or other unusual features).

Paxton checked 'personally viewed' and filled in most of the blanks. "I don't know his service number."

Ferko hooked his finger through the chain around Casey's neck, pulled out his dog tags, and read Paxton the number to copy. Then, still reading, he said, "Ah, and he's actually Elkiah no-middle-name Jones."

"We always just called him Casey."

"Happens quite often, Sergeant." They corrected the name on the form, Paxton circled 'facial features' and Ferko closed the bag.

Kessler's next. Has to be.

Ferko absently pushed his glasses higher on the bridge of his nose, unzipped the third bag and pushed the flaps to the sides. His skin was the color of putty. The left eye was gone, along with most of that side of his face and head. But the right eye showed fully, locked in an odd-angled stare at the dimmer reaches of the ceiling. He walked slowly around the gurney. In profile from the right, Kessler, though lifeless, was clearly Kessler. From the left, however, this was one of the anonymous dead, literally faceless. His shredded left ear and the portion of his head that it clung to had vanished in transit. His skull lay open and largely empty, though a generous smear of brain had spilled out and spread across the bottom of the body bag. Red ants trekked across the inside wall of the skull, plying their humdrum trade, although they were difficult to see because they were shaded. He looked up at the ceiling fixtures and rubbed his hand across his eyes. It seemed to him that dark rather than light was streaming from the fluorescents, cascades of shadow were spilling down impersonally onto the living and the dead.

Hey, Kessler, this is the place.

"Oh, no," Ferko said, looking at Kessler's head. "Nonviewable. No, out of the question."

"Nonviewable?" Paxton repeated, not comprehending.

Again Ferko's eyes focused on nothing. "Restoration to a normal, lifelike appearance not possible. Extensive disfigurement, extreme mutilation, advanced stages of decomposition, severe burning. Suicides. Floaters. Viewable surfaces charred or burned. Homicides." His eyes slowly returned to their current surroundings and he looked at the gurneys all around him. "Yes," he murmured. "Homicides."

He searched for Kessler's dog tags in vain. Whatever had removed the left third of his skull and face had also severed the chain around his neck. The tags were somewhere under 15 inches of paddy water. Ferko looked perplexed at their absence. "I know him," Paxton said, and filled in the entire form, right down to Kessler's service number. He could also have given him the serial number of Kessler's M16, if he'd needed it. Paxton prided himself on knowing both numbers for every man in his squad. Between casualties and normal rotation, that meant 19 men so far. At this point in time, however, it didn't feel like a particularly desirable accomplishment. A name, a number, a body—three kinds of identifiers. *But where's Kessler?*

As Ferko closed the bag, he glanced at the next gurney in the line. Paxton noticed some writing on the outside of the body bag—'Godspeed,' and 'Thanks, Doc,' and 'You saved my life.' But Ferko was focused on something else—the zipper on that body bag had not been completely shut and four darkish white slugs had spilled out and were writhing slowly on the gurney's surface, leaving intermittent trails of slime in their wake.

"Oh," Ferko said, plainly indignant. "Maggots. Unacceptable." He clutched the clipboard to his breast and his eyes locked on nothing. "Maggots and other parasites shall be destroyed, removed and their breeding sites on the body thoroughly treated. Sufficient time must be allowed to permit the fumes from chemical preparations used in killing parasites and larvae to dissipate, in order to prevent the accumulation of odors." His eyes returned and fell on a tag tied to the bag. Incredulous at its presence, he read it. "Oh, this is unconscionable!" He looked around. "Major Boykins!" he called. "Just look at these remains here."

The Major left the two soldiers he was talking to and came over.

"Look, Major. Maggots." He pointed to them.

"It happens, Mister Ferko. You know that."

"But these remains aren't raw from the field." He angrily brandished the tag attached to the bag. "They came through a Graves Registration Point, and they came through like this!" He zipped open the bag to show a mud-smeared face under close-cropped brown hair. Through the half-open shirt, they could see a small colony of larvae at vigorous work in a chest wound.

"Close the bag, please, Mister Ferko," the Major said evenly. Ferko did so with an angry flourish and then turned back to the Major.

"I believe it serves no purpose to transport dirt and maggots halfway across Vietnam." His voice was almost too low to understand the words. He was clearly working hard to control himself. "I believe it is a small enough gesture of respect to clean the face of the remains and make an effort to remove vermin and other insects from him prior to his shipment." Without ever raising his voice, Ferko's indignation had escalated into outrage. "Major Boykins, this requires a letter through command channels."

The Major looked at his watch. "All right, Mister Ferko," he said wearily. "Let's go to my office and we'll talk about our options."

They set off briskly, oblivious of Paxton. He followed uncertainly after them for a few steps, then halted in the middle of the large room as they pushed through a set of swinging doors, windowed like the kitchen doors of a restaurant, and disappeared. Behind him he heard the sound of gurneys on the move and turned to see the Vietnamese workers pushing the eight sets of remains. All the bodies were in motion, coming toward him at a steady pace, a surreal, inexorable procession of American dead and oriental acolytes. He froze as they came nearer, then swirled around him and finally passed him on either side. The workers paid him no heed at all. He had the odd sensation that he must be invisible.

They followed after Ferko and the Major. The doors slapped back and forth a few times, and then went still. Paxton walked over to them.

Through the window, he could see the Vietnamese and a number of GIs and American civilians, some in lab coats, transferring the dead from the body bags to work tables. Ten in all, the tables sloped down toward sinks. Each station had a pump-like device beside it on the floor and a stainless steel waste can with a pedal-operated lid. On the opposite wall, five walk-in reefers were lined up, enough room for probably 25 or 30 cadavers. Paxton wondered how many bodies they processed in a day. *Depends on the day.* On the door of the middle reefer a large stenciled sign read 'Human Remains Only.' Directly below the letters, by way of explanation, was a large, bold scrawl: 'No Food.' Although standard fluorescents lit the room, the sun poured through another set of double doors in the workroom wall to Paxton's right.

Kessler already rested on one of the tables and an American was swiftly cutting away his uniform, boots and all. In seconds, he lay naked. Paxton looked from his penis to his gaping skull. Showing one's exposed genitals to all and sundry in the showers was a normal condition of life in Vietnam, routinely reciprocated and hardly thought about. But to have one's skull laid open and its contents spilled and scattered—to Paxton, that was so grossly, viciously obscene, a condition so offensive that he had to avert his eyes and turn away.

A Vietnamese worker began pushing the gurney with Kessler's body bag and stretcher toward the sunlit doors. Paxton looked around. The room he was in also had an entryway leading outside.

As he pushed through and out, Kessler's gurney emerged ten yards farther on. He and the worker stood on the loading dock, looking down at the concrete hardstand that sloped to a sewer grating in the middle. Another Vietnamese was at work near the drain, hosing blood and other renderings off stretchers and out of body bags. The worker on the dock dropped Kessler's body bag and stretcher down onto the hardstand, then pushed the gurney past Paxton and back into the building. Paxton watched in a kind of suspended animation, as the other worker finished the pieces of equipment at hand, set them aside to dry in the sun and brought Kessler's to the sewer.

Holding the hose, he stood in full sunlight out on the concrete, wearing only a pair of black shorts that had become soaked during his chores. In shadow on the loading dock, Paxton shrank back even farther against the wall, as the worker started wetting down Kessler's stretcher.

The canvas required only cursory attention because the body bag had retained the spills and seepages of Kessler's dying. The worker pulled the bag over to the sewer, turned it half inside out and began a thorough hosing. The water turned a light but unmistakable pink against the whitish concrete and flushed out little globules of tissue, some strands of viscous matter and a small, roughly square patch of filmy membrane. When the water ran clear again, he pulled the body bag aside and set about methodically flushing the scattered remnants into the sewer. A few hours before, these bits of flesh had held Kessler's growing hope that he would reach the end of his tour intact. Now Paxton watched as they vanished slowly down the openings in the grate. The worker briefly played the hose on each of his bare feet, crossed to the spigot, turned it off and went into the building by the far door.

Paxton stared for long seconds at the sewer, then eased himself down off the loading dock, walked slowly to the grating and knelt down. He laid his rifle on the concrete and, leaning back on his heels, hands on thighs, forced himself to think back to the ambush.

The initiating explosion had to be a claymore, a heavy charge of plastic explosive embedded with hundreds of metal projectiles. Kessler stood directly between him and the claymore, and took the full brunt of the shrapnel. He died instantly, while Paxton, shielded by him, had gone untouched.

He rolled forward on all fours, grasping hold of the grate, and peered into its depths. He wanted to glimpse Kessler one last time to tell him something, but found himself unable to put his feelings into words. He felt Kessler's presence strongly, just beyond the light, and wanted to touch him, embrace him. But he also sensed the yawning divide between them now, the steel grate its pale shadow. That gap—its immensity, its utter finality—broke upon him, intensified, and finally pushed aside his urgent need to penetrate it. It overwhelmed all his resistance to it, giving him no choice. It simply *was*, oblivious of Paxton and his needs. His head sank down and he moaned, slumping over into a sitting position. He clung shakily to the grate with one hand, while the other covered his eyes to protect them from the painful brightness pressing down on the hardstand. When he looked again, tiny flecks of ash were drifting downward like a delicate fall of snow.

Sewers and chimneys, sewers and chimneys.

He's gone.

Something in him wanted to resist. They'd slept beside each other on paddy dikes and in foxholes. The first time Paxton was wounded, his leg peppered by grenade fragments, Kessler had bandaged it. And now he was gone? He looked into the sewer's mouth. What does that mean, Gone? Is it a location, a coordinate on a map? *Place of the weird geography.* He laid his hand over his pocket and felt the bottle of pills through the cloth.

As weird as Vietnam was, it was still geography. He stood up and looked around. The mortuary occupied an L-shaped building, with the concrete pad sitting in the angle where the two wings joined. He guessed that the hardstand didn't just cover a rock-filled sump, because the smell would soon drive everyone away. He looked out across the terrain. The sewer had to go somewhere, had to access some watercourse that would carry off the leavings of the dead. And that's where Gone is, Paxton decided with a grim smile, at the other end of this sewer line. The Gone where Kessler's gotten to.

Once he started looking for it, the track where the sewer's ditch had been dug became obvious, a slight depression in the land running straight and undeviating to a ragged line of nipa palm a quarter of a mile away. So Gone sits in a clump of nipa. Might have known. He retrieved his rifle and soon arrived at the tree line.

Gone, he found, was a place of green shadows, relative coolness and ominous quiet. Although it was scored by a lattice of worn paths, it was currently deserted. A little trickle of a stream meandered through at roughly right angles to the sewer line. In a matter of moments, he found where the drain emptied into it about 20 feet away. He looked back through the green air at the distant mortuary and saw the worker resuming his place in the center of the brilliant tropical sunlight.

He waited, for what he wasn't sure. What was he doing here, really? Gone is gone, a condition, not a location—and for Kessler, a permanent one. It slowly dawned on him that Gone was every empty place Kessler no longer filled. More than that: as they'd walked the paddies, Kessler had duplicated himself cell by cell inside Paxton, and that was the place where his absence was most acute. No map coordinates there, the only actual place of the weird geography.

But then what was this feeling? Where Kessler had been there was an intense feeling—discovered and contemplated while resting in green shadows. Trying to grasp that feeling brought back memories and emotions from his track days in high school. The training and conditioning, the competition, finding physical capabilities in himself he hadn't known existed. He remembered the day he ran the third leg of a relay race, took the baton and kicked out with a swiftness and intensity that none of his practices had ever shown him. He ran absolutely full bore and came to the handoff to Lloyd Grove with nothing left. But Lloyd launched a split second early and there was a moment, a fraction of a moment, when losing the baton was a real possibility and Paxton, empty, found a little more and made the handoff. And the whole sequence had happened in decimals of a second, followed immediately by sweet victory—triumph, the realization that together they had done it. He reveled in the camaraderie and basked in the knowledge that he had overcome real obstacles, had arrived at the end of the race more than he had been at the beginning.

A thin stream of water began trickling out of the sewer and pattering onto a pile of white rocks, deliberately stacked under the pipe to prevent erosion. What he felt now about Kessler contained all of those feelings sustaining the memory of his jock days, but those feelings alone were inadequate to fully illuminate his emotions now. What occupied Kessler's place inside him now was deeper, more somber and complex. And so it had been, he realized, even while Kessler lived. The word *love* came to him, without any sexual connotation, and waited patiently, it seemed, for him to process it. His mind fluttered tentatively away from the word, in obedience to the conditioned responses he had absorbed in the locker rooms of his jock triumphs. But the palpable presence of death overcame the synthetic rules and cleared the way for a simple insight. He loved Kessler, and as long as he lived he would never forget him. But then a stab of pain hit his stomach, as he realized Kessler had gone out in the field with him and met his fate because of Paxton. *Send your best…*

He looked back at the sewer. The water had turned a delicate pink against the white rocks, but this time Paxton was not surprised. Nor was he surprised when a strand of unidentifiable human flesh flowed half out of the sewer opening, caught, and hung there waiting for a surge of water to push it back on its journey. Rather, he found himself weary, worn down by these views of mortality that were normally kept behind opaque plastic sheeting, to avoid evoking the ultimate risk of combat.

That risk, it seemed to him, was the only difference between jocking and combat that really mattered. Every troop who processed into Vietnam signed his life away—every single one. Death had the option of collecting or not, and nobody could ever know why this one was foreclosed and not that one, why Kessler was dead and not Paxton. But from the day-in, day-out sharing of that risk had grown the single intuitive reality—his feelings for Kessler. Paxton hoped that when the emotional dust settled, he would feel more grateful that Kessler had saved his life and less guilty that it had cost Kessler his own to do it. But he knew, inside this present moment at least, that both the gratitude and the guilt were rooted in love. *Yes,* Paxton thought, consenting to it, thankful for it. *Yes, I love Kessler.* But across this simple emotional truth the dark shadow fell again: *It's my fault.*

He caught a movement at the sewer vent out of the corner of his eye. When he looked, he saw that the water had almost stopped and the strand of human flesh was swinging, pendulum-like, back and forth. But that's not what had moved. Something gray shifted inside the pile of white stones. Had the breeze stirred a scrap of paper? The strand hung still now, straight down. Then, even as he watched, a dark gray something shot up out of the white rocks and fell back, leaving the dangling piece swinging again, an inch shorter.

A rat.

His belly roiled, as he realized that rats were violating the remains of soldiers killed in battle, browsing through them like garbage. In a split second, his anger was fully formed. He seethed with rage, sensed it deepen without bottoming out.

But at the same time that he nurtured it, he kept it under rigid control. His instinct was to chop up the gray body with a magazine of M16 on full automatic, turn it into shreds of food for its own kind, like his squad had done with the pack of dogs. But he knew the rat was too small, and that the shot pattern of the M16 on automatic would be too broad. Maybe with a single shot. He locked a fresh magazine into his rifle and chambered a round. But then he realized that a ricochet off the pile of stones could go anywhere, carrying as far as the populated areas of the garrison or even coming back at himself. He reluctantly put the weapon on safety, looked around and picked up a stone a little smaller than a baseball. He leaned his rifle against a palm and waited for the rat.

When he saw patches of gray stirring among the shadows in the pile of stones, he tensed and cocked his arm back. From behind him, something grabbed his wrist and shook the stone easily from his grasp. Paxton whirled instinctively, ready to go hand to hand—or at least tried to whirl. But his wrist was tightly gripped by a fist the size of a catcher's mitt, attached to a man towering over Paxton as much as he had towered above Ferko. An American, he wore civilian clothes—shorts, T-shirt and sneakers without socks. He stood at least six-six and must have weighed 275 pounds. Feeling quite helpless, Paxton began wondering what this prominent terrain feature would do with him. The man slapped a .45-caliber pistol into his hand and released him.

The big man's mouth twisted into a conspiratorial grin, his eyes tightened to slits and he whispered, "Snake shot."

"What?"

"It's loaded with snake shot," he said. "Like a shotgun round for pistols." He paused a second for emphasis and added, "No ricochets."

As he grasped the implications, Paxton's face lit up. He slid the safety off and turned back to the sewer vent, just in time to squeeze off a round at the rat as it sprang upward out of the rocks and made a pass at the dangling strand. The force of the shot knocked it off the pile of stones. It hit the ground hard, rolled completely over and sprang up, moving in a shaky run to a hole in the embankment a little beyond the sewer.

"Hey! Nice shot." The big man grinned.

"It got away."

"Not clean, it didn't. You drew blood."

"I want the fucker dead."

"We're a little too far back. The shot scatter's too broad to bring it down."

"What's maximum effective range?"

"For snake shot? About ten feet." Paxton gave him a skeptical look. "No, really. Get much farther away than the end of their tail and you're in trouble."

The sewer flow started again, this time a deeper color that went distinctly toward red.

"Uh oh," the big man said. "They're embalming up there. Five quarts of blood in the human body and it all has to come out. They cut it with the water they use to flush it, but it's still pretty potent when it gets here. Look for the rats. They'll catch the smell of it in a second."

Paxton looked beyond the pile of rocks, the way the rat had gone.

"No, the other way," the big man corrected him. "Downstream."

He turned and saw another big gray on the other side of the water at its edge, snout up and testing the wind. Paxton started moving to close the distance.

"Whoa," the big man said, and grabbed him by the collar. "That's Numero Uno," he explained. "First among filthy equals, smartest of the smart. He watches like a hawk. You'll never get close enough to pop him. I've never seen him blink."

The red flow was emerging from under the pile of white rocks. When it hit the trickle of the stream, the color change was immediate, like a muddy river emptying into a clear one. The line between the two shades of the stream was unmistakable and Paxton, fascinated, watched its progress toward Numero Uno. As the line drew close, the big gray edged forward until its front paws were in the water, and when it passed him he began to drink.

Paxton's anger surged again, still not bottoming out. The rat was nourishing itself on the blood of soldiers, extracting it from the thin trickle of water. Pure rage swirled inside him. Paxton swore to himself that he would perform any task, take any risk to kill this obscene thing. Without lifting its muzzle from the flow, the rat turned its red eyes on Paxton, as if to mock his resolve.

"Stay where he can see you, but don't spook him," Paxton told the big man. "I'm going to kill the son of a bitch."

Paxton went prone and pushed into a dense clump of nipa, knotted and tangled in a thick undergrowth of vines. When he fully extended his arm, he couldn't see his hand. He didn't think he'd run into any snakes. The network of paths indicated a frequent human presence, and the snakes didn't like people any more than people liked them. But he'd have to be careful.

It was only 20 feet to the water, but it would take a minute or two because he'd have to move slowly so as not to startle the big gray back into its hole. But he couldn't take all day. Once the rat had its fill, it would be gone. He'd have to get up to the water's edge, not only because of the shot scatter, but because the vegetation was so thick he wouldn't be able to see the rat till he was virtually on top of it.

The vines grabbed and tangled around him and he had to tear some of them apart with his hands to get through. Rocks scraped his forearms as he crawled along, and stray branches poked at him from odd angles. As he shoved hard through a wedge of thick green, he was stung sharply on his left arm and thought for a second that it was indeed a snake. But he'd pushed his bandaged wound directly into the pointed end of a dead branch. The pain was intense and hung on stubbornly. When he looked, drops of blood were accumulating below the bandage and inching down his arm. He cursed silently, with deep feeling. Should have left the sleeve on the shirt, he thought, and hoped he hadn't torn any of the sutures under the bandage. He didn't want to have to get stitched up again. He pushed on.

Soon, his fatigue shirt was soaked with sweat and sticking to his back. He didn't think he had much farther to go, but he didn't know how much longer the big gray would linger. And then he began to see glimpses of the opposite bank through the greenery. In another 18 inches, he spied the rat sitting at the water's edge, regarding the big man coolly.

Paxton judged the range to be about eight feet. Feasible, but he still wanted to shorten it. He wanted to be absolutely sure. He got another foot closer and then, as he tried for more, the rat's head turned sharply in his direction, the red eyes trying to penetrate the green. *Got to do it now.* Moving deliberately, he aligned the rear sight aperture and the front sight blade on the rat, just as it moved nervously a foot to the left, ready for flight. Paxton heard the big man address the rat softly: "Hey, filthy rat—look at me, sweetie. Stay put, now."

It stayed, its attention distracted by the big man just long enough for Paxton to realign his sights. He picked a spot a bit forward of its middle and, squeezing carefully, opened a wound behind its shoulder the size of a nickel. The force of the shot knocked it sideways three inches and rolled it over, dead.

"Nice one!" The big man yelled excitedly. "Greased him, by God!"

Paxton stood up and crossed over to where the rat lay.

"I want to tell you, that was good shooting." The big man was beaming and shook his head admiringly. "You've got to be a combat troop to stalk like that," he said.

Arms akimbo, Paxton stood triumphant over the rat. He toed it once, then again. The rat's body was flaccid and yielding. It was Paxton's to do with as he pleased. That's for you, Matt, he told Kessler. At once, enormous waves of pain shot through his arm at the wound, radiating upward across his shoulder and into his neck. At the same time, it rushed downward through his forearm and into his hand until every finger and joint throbbed with an excess of hurting. Then it pushed upward from his neck and over his skull. He felt as if someone was tightening a steel band around his head. The big man came up to him and retrieved the pistol, grinning and talking, but Paxton couldn't hear any words. There was just moving lips. A wave of nausea and dizziness swept over him. He grabbed hold of the other to steady himself, and the big man, concerned, hung onto him. After a few moments, his balance and then his hearing returned, but he was enormously weak. The big man walked him to a fallen tree and sat him down.

"You all right now?" he asked.

A thin trickle of blood extended from his wound all the way to his elbow, and another drop was starting down as he looked. He needed another pill, but his watch said he had two more hours to wait. *Fuck it.* He pulled the bottle out of his pocket.

"Are you all right?" the big man repeated.

Paxton was in a struggle to get the lid off the bottle, and losing. The fingers of his left hand felt thick and numb. He could hardly close them around the medicine. "Can you get me a pill out of here?"

He did. As Paxton put it in his mouth, the big man slid the bottle back into Paxton's pocket and pulled the canteen off his pistol belt.

He washed the pill down with a long drag of hot canteen water, then slumped forward a little and closed his eyes.

"Did you know you're bleeding?" the big man asked as he capped the canteen and tucked it back into Paxton's belt.

Did he ever. "Yeah," Paxton said, wincing as he chuckled. He told him about getting his wound sutured at the hospital and identifying his KIAs. It never occurred to him to talk about the firefight.

"That's where I work," the big man said, gesturing with his head toward the mortuary, "and I've got a bottle of just the medicine you need, up in my locker. Some real smooth Canadian stuff." The sun hung behind the big man, outlining his head with a warm golden glow that shifted to a radiant dark green at its outer edges.

"I don't think I..."

"I'm Harry Cassidy, by the way, but everybody calls me Hopalong—after those old westerns, you know?" He took Paxton's hand and shook it.

Paxton squinted against the halo of light around the other. "Chuck Paxton," he said, smiling weakly. He wondered if all the undertakers up there were compulsive hand shakers.

"I just got off shift. Like to come down here and pop a few rats to unwind. We do a ten-hour shift, but when we're done we spend a couple of hours cleaning up and resupplying the work stations for the next bunch." Paxton thought of the tables tilting down toward the sinks. "So by the time we're done, it's a twelve-hour day. Who'd you work with up there?"

"A guy named Ferko."

"Oh, yeah, George. He just came on duty. Good man, George. Nice guy, really dedicated. But *little*—short and skinny," the big man said. "Hey. You feeling better?"

"Yeah, some."

"Come on, Chuck. I'll take you up and medicate you."

Paxton retrieved his rifle, then turned for a last look at the rat. It was gone, and he stiffened, alarmed. "Where'd the damned thing go?"

"Rat heaven, where else?"

"No, where's it at? It was right over there on the other bank."

"You kicked it into the water. Didn't you? I thought you did." He turned back briefly and looked around.

Paxton knew the rat was dead. He knew it as soon as the shot hit it, and he confirmed it when he mocked it with his boot, standing over the filthy gray, flaunting his victory. But where was it? He was sure he hadn't kicked it into the water. Or had he? Maybe in that dizzy spell? The stream's flow was still reddish, but glowed now as if lit from below. The light shining up was a gleaming black, an anti-light, turning the water to a luminescent red, marbled with radiant shadow. He wondered what was in those pills. He scanned the water downstream as far as he could see, without success. If the rat's on the loose...no, it's dead. But he had the feeling he was trying to convince himself and botching it. Reluctantly, he admitted he was afraid.

He checked the stream once more. Just underwater, he noticed a strand of human tissue draped over a submerged branch. His mouth dropped open. Right next to the branch was a small smooth stone that wasn't a stone at all but an eye, Kessler's eyeball rocking gently on the bottom. And then a short distance away, he saw Kessler's ear, shredded but still hanging together and recognizable. *Weird geography, place of the weird...* Trying to appear relaxed, he laid his hand casually over the bandage and slowly jammed his index finger into it with increasing pressure. The wound protested with new waves of pain that made him light-headed for a few seconds. Fresh blood began to seep out from under the bandage. When he looked into the water again, the pieces of anatomy were gone. The stream shimmered red and deep black.

"Come on, time for four fingers of Hopalong's potion." Paxton briefly ran a hand across his eyes, as if trying to wipe away a spider's web he'd just walked through in deep forest. The big man laid a huge hand on his right shoulder and steered him gently along a path back toward the mortuary.

"Don't worry about the rat," he said. "That shot of yours left him real dead. I love to come down here and pop those goddam things, you know? They're filthy. Took the pistol off a Marine lieutenant when he came through up there. He sure didn't need it anymore, and I think I'm putting it to pretty good use if I do say so. Snake shot tears hell out of it, though, no good now for standard ammo without a new barrel. But it's gonna be snake shot for the foreseeable, I can tell you that—as long as I'm in country."

The big man went on nonstop, all the way back to the mortuary. When he took Paxton into the admin section of the building, they found Ferko talking to two aviators. Probably came to identify the dead pilot, Paxton decided. And then he recognized young Garrett Prue, the warrant officer who flew slicks for them sometimes. At the same moment, Garrett saw Paxton.

"Major Tolliver," Mister Prue said. "Here's Sergeant Paxton."

The major was probably the commander of the gunship company. He came toward Paxton with a big smile, looking like he was about to offer his hand, but caught sight of the track of drying blood down Paxton's left arm.

"You pick this up today?"

"Yes, sir," Paxton answered. "They sewed it up over at the hospital and then I came here to identify my people."

"Same route we took," said the Major.

"We saw Baker right after they took his foot off," Mister Prue added. Paxton's eyes flicked over to Ferko for a moment, but he remained impassive.

"He was pretty groggy, but he told us about the firefight," the Major said.

Paxton assumed he meant getting his people caught in an ambush and all the casualties. His face reddened, and his eyes faltered. "It was pretty ugly out there for a while," he mumbled.

"He said you dragged him across two rice paddies under heavy fire."

Paxton realized then that he wasn't in trouble. "Did he tell you that when I got hit, he pulled himself over to me with his leg like that and tied pieces of his bootlace together to make a tourniquet? You should put him in for a medal, sir."

He smiled. "I will, Sergeant Paxton, I will."

"Baker told us you lost some other people," Mister Prue said. "Sounds like it was pretty bad."

"Yeah," Paxton replied. "Matt Kessler, my RTO, and Casey Jones from second squad."

"I knew Kessler."

"But they never found Ken Janowitz's body out there. I don't know why."

"Janowitz?" Mister Prue seemed stunned by the news.

"Yeah. He was in the rear of the patrol when they sprang the ambush up front. Then, when he tried to catch up to the rest of us, an RPG round went off right under his feet."

Major Tolliver looked at his watch. "We need to hit the road, Garrett. We'll close in a bit after dark, as it is." He turned to Paxton. "Where are you headed?"

"I wanted to get back to Bearcat, but I'll probably have to overnight here." He gave a tight little smile. "Top told me to get wasted."

"If you still want to get back, we'll drop you," the Major said. "It's right on our way back to base."

"What, flying?"

"Sure."

That suited Paxton just fine. He didn't think the booze would be able to shut down the day's memories before he got unconscious. Besides, he was well past wanting to get wasted. He hurt in every bone and muscle of his body. All he wanted now was to sleep.

He sat in the door of the helicopter, feet dangling just above the skid, looking down on the random patchwork of rice paddies, green nipa, villages and firebases, all wired together by slender highways and vague dirt tracks. The setting was deceptively serene. With darkness, the NVA would stalk the land, made bold by the concealment of the night. At the same time, the stalkers would be stalked by friendlies and the two sides would dance their murderous little dance until one of them made some fatal error. The peaceful picture far below him, touched with the light of the setting sun, was lying. Even now, the killing continued and would only intensify with the night.

He felt at the moment like the land—outwardly peaceful and at rest, inwardly disturbed. He knew he'd taken out the rat. Yet, its disappearance by the sewer left him deeply troubled. Part of him acknowledged it was silly—dead is dead, and with that gaping hole in its side it was very much deceased. But another part of him found it impossible to shake off the thought of that endless stream of GIs going into the mortuary. They're carried in, ripped and broken, then go through some industrial process that makes them presentable at home. How had Ferko put it in one of those little trances? Restored to a normal, lifelike appearance, that was it. Or else declared officially nonviewable. But there's a third category here. What about the Kesslers, so torn, so shredded, that not the most finely meshed screen in the world could keep the tattered wreckage of their bodies from the rat? The anger returned when he thought of the big gray nourishing itself on the flesh and blood of dead soldiers.

And that rat. What if it's dead but not dead? What if it continues on, no matter how big the hole in its side? Where did it go with those red eyes? What would he have to do to keep it from its obscene feast?

Whatever it takes. He made that promise to Kessler. *Whatever it takes.*

CHAPTER 4

When he got to his cantonment area in Bearcat, the troops were cleaned up and in formation on the company street. Captain Bonner was talking and the Padre was standing by. Three M16s with fixed bayonets were stuck fast in the earth, muzzles down, each topped by a helmet and with a pair of combat boots beside it. They had Casey Jones' helmet, with his ace of spades tucked in the retainer band. Apparently, they'd even found Janowitz's helmet, with the P-38 for opening cans of C rations wedged under the band. But the one for Kessler wasn't Kessler's at all. It had a brand new camouflage cover and had to be right out of the supply room. Paxton decided the real one wasn't presentable.

He looked over at the third platoon, his platoon. First squad consisted of Al Gomez as acting squad leader, and Schiller. *Send your best...* He decided not to join the formation. His boots and pants were filthy, the left sleeve was ripped out of his shirt, his wounded arm was crusted with blood, and he needed a shower. Captain Bonner was saying something about

18 enemy KIAs, and Paxton was glad. But then he looked back at his two-man squad. *It isn't worth it.*

Hardly anyone realized he'd returned, and he preferred it that way. He was at the far side of the formation, and everyone was focused on the Old Man. But Padre on the other side caught his eye and, without making a big deal out of it, flashed him one of his smiles. Then the Old Man introduced the priest.

Padre kept it personal and low key. He talked about Kessler and the Kool-Aid his mother sent him, and Casey Jones and his ham and lima beans. Then he mentioned Janowitz's coolness in his first big firefight when he assumed the leadership role and called in artillery, holding him out as a model to follow.

Then he quoted something from the Old Testament. "Consider, oh Israel," he intoned, "for them that are dead: David the King mourned and wept and fasted until evening because they were fallen by the sword. And the King made this lamentation: How are the valiant fallen in battle? How are the valiant fallen? They were swifter than eagles, stronger than lions. How are the valiant fallen?" He tied that into the centurion who wanted Jesus to cure his dying servant. "This Roman soldier," Padre said, "had Jesus all figured out because he told Jesus he *too* was subject to authority. It's as if he knew that Jesus' chain of command ran straight to the Father and he had to obey, even if it meant the cross," Padre said. "To my mind, Jesus was a soldier when he obeyed the Father's command and ended up on Calvary, a KIA just like the men we're remembering. And no soldier who's been in the combat of Calvary will leave Janowitz and Kessler and Casey Jones out in the dark places." He ended up back in the Old Testament: "Mine eye spared them and destroyed them not, neither did I make an end of them in the wilderness. And when I gather you out of the countries wherein you have been scattered, I will embrace you and I will be sanctified in you before the heathen."

As Padre finished and began putting on the vestments for the mass, Doc Watson, one of the company medics, came up to Paxton and immediately began checking his wound. Sometimes Paxton would occasionally fake a British accent and call him Doctor Watson, and then they'd string together some Sherlock Holmes patter that gave them a few laughs.

"I've got to tell you, Sarge, you look like shit," Doc said cheerfully. "Did you go kill some more gooks after they put this on?"

"No. I went on safari."

Doc pulled out a gauze packet and tore open the wrapper. "On safari, huh?" He started cleaning off some of the blood.

"Yeah. Hunting rats."

"Big game, huh? Did you get any?"

"Yeah. Well, I think so. I'm not sure."

"Dead is dead."

"I hope so."

"Most of this stuff is crusted hard already. Let's go over to the aid station. I'll clean you up right and give you a fresh dressing."

"I'll be over in a bit. I want to stick around for Padre's mass."

"Suit yourself. I'll be around." He wandered off.

They had piled up cases of hand grenades into two adjoining stacks to form a makeshift altar. Paxton idly wondered if the grenades would land with more accuracy after the mass was said over them. He smiled at that a bit, but the melancholy refused to subside.

It was full dark now, the end of a very long day. Perhaps 20 people had stayed behind for the mass. Someone pulled a jeep up to the opposite side of the grenade cases, so the headlights would provide illumination. When the engine was cut off, the lights dimmed a couple of notches and then settled into their new cruising level.

Padre finished vesting by slipping a chasuble over his head. The vestment looked to be made from upscale camouflage cloth, its sheen making it appear brand new. Because of that, it seemed out of place, like the helmet they had put out for Kessler. When Chaplain McCurdy gave everyone general absolution, Paxton crossed himself.

The priest took his place at the altar, which tilted slightly down toward Paxton. He had to squint against the headlights to see Chaplain McCurdy, who'd become a shadow priest. "In the name of the Father, and of the Son, and of the Holy Spirit," Padre began. Paxton shifted his position a bit so he wouldn't have to look directly into the headlights, but the priest remained a silhouette.

He tried to follow along for a few minutes, then gave it up. His mind seemed to have its own agenda, ranging across the events of the day. It touched just long enough on his encounter with Red and her offer to rate the event of little importance. He surprised himself by readily agreeing. Both the firefight and the visit to the mortuary were more crucial happenings. But the visit seemed to have the edge, perhaps because it was more recent. Or perhaps because his mind's eye began to bring up the image of Kessler lying naked on the table, and superimposing him on the makeshift altar.

"I will wash my hands among the innocent..."

Paxton felt his mouth go dry and his pulse rate pick up. He willed the sight of Kessler away, ordered it to leave, pleaded with it without success.

"Father, receive this sacrifice at our hands..."

It was only as he began to reach up with studied casualness toward his wound that the vision finally started to fade.

But waiting behind it lay another image. Beads of sweat gathered on his forehead as he watched the rat drinking at the stream, front paws in the bloodied water, red eyes mocking him. As this waking dream of the rat intensified, Padre bent over the shadow bread, softly saying the words that brought God. He raised the offering toward heaven. As he spoke over the shadow cup, Paxton, eyes riveted on the rat, jammed his fingers with a kind of controlled panic into the dressing that covered his wound. The desperate pain washed over him while Padre raised the chalice. At last, the rat began to fade. Soon, only a shadow priest in camouflage was left, praying at a makeshift altar.

Paxton's whole arm pulsed with pain. Bone weary, he pulled out the bottle of pills and managed to wrench off the cover. He downed the tablet with the last of his canteen water and sank to his knees, exhausted.

While they prayed the Our Father together right before communion, Paxton covered his eyes for a moment against the light and the weariness. "And lead us not into temptation but deliver us from evil." As he took his hand away, he caught sight of a blur of dark gray behind the front wheel of the jeep. This was no waking dream, no return to the mortuary, no set-piece illusion. This was walking through his reality. Tensing, he shaded his eyes against the headlights, searching the ground under the jeep. As he peered into the darkness, a pair of small red eyes moved out from behind the tire and stared back at him, defying him. Padre picked up the small golden plate and held one of the wafers above the other pieces of altar bread. "Behold the Lamb of God, behold Him Who takes away the sins of the world." The rat emerged from the darkness behind the tire and moved deliberately toward the stacked cases. It brazenly turned so that Paxton could see the nickel-sized hole in its left side, and then vanished behind the altar.

The sight of the wound stunned Paxton. Until he saw the gaping hole he was convinced it was a different rat. Now one part of him believed he was hallucinating. Had to be. Another part of him knew with a gut certainty that the rat, wound and all, lived in his here and now, and was proving that Paxton's best efforts couldn't keep it from its obscene banquet.

A brief flash of dark gray showed on the altar itself before disappearing. Paxton looked desperately at Padre for help. The shadow priest stood with his back to the altar, facing the congregation and holding the shadow bread in his hand. "Lord, I am not worthy to receive you..." Paxton looked back at the cases of grenades. The rat sat atop them next to the gaping head of Kessler, who lay naked and defenseless on the altar.

"Paxton."

It was demonstrating its absolute freedom to do whatever it wanted with the dead.

"Paxton?"

Chaplain McCurdy was gesturing to him to come and be the first to receive communion. He seemed dazed as Padre said, "Body of Christ." First, the priest placed the wafer on his tongue, then reached back and picked up the chalice off the altar. Kessler still lay helpless, but the rat had willfully hidden itself again, playing with Paxton, intensifying his fears. But when he took the chalice from Padre to sip the consecrated wine, everything became clear. "Blood of Christ." The transparent face of the rat shimmered deep in the amber cup. The red eyes dared him to drain the chalice.

Paxton knew his choices—drink, or watch the rat return to Kessler. He brought the cup to his lips and drank long slow swallows until his eyes were looking up at the base of the chalice. Someone in the little congregation laughed nervously as Doc Watson eased in beside him. Still dazed, Paxton brought the cup down from his mouth, and Padre gently took it from him. Doc Watson slid his arm around his shoulder. "Come on, Sarge," he said. "Let's go sit down."

Doc Watson walked him away from the glaring headlights and into the dark. Later, he medicated him for the night and then talked with him the next morning. Doc was no shrink, but he knew what to listen for. In the afternoon, they evacuated Paxton to the hospital in Saigon.

That evening the hospital fed him, and that night a nurse medicated him again. She couldn't seem to decide between being cheery or awesomely competent. When she told him to take the capsule, she was brusque to the point of severity. Once he'd swallowed it, she gave him an instant wall-to-wall smile. She told him he'd see Doctor Brinker in the morning and be back at his company before the day was out.

That night Paxton slept, but it wasn't restful.

☽

In the morning, Paxton found himself sitting in front of the desk of Major George Harlan Brinker, M.D.

"A rat?" the Doctor asked.

Paxton nodded.

"Can you describe it for me?" Doctor Brinker wore a lab coat over his fatigues, and had put a major's leaves on the white lapel. Paxton's file was open in front of him on the desk.

"He's about this long," Paxton replied, holding his hands a foot apart.

"Including the tail?" That confused Paxton.

"Well—no, he's..." Paxton added another seven or eight inches to his imaginary rat. "With the tail, he's about this long."

"What color?"

"Dark gray, going toward black."

"Anything else?"

Paxton glanced out the open window for a second. As he pictured the rat on the makeshift altar, his brow furrowed. "The eyes—they were red. Tight little red eyes he had." Paxton focused on the rat in his mind. "A mean face. Vicious."

Paxton looked like he was on the verge of adding more details, so the doctor left him in his recollection for a moment. But nothing else came. "That it?" the doctor asked.

Paxton's gaze slid to the floor beside him, seeing nothing,

remembering. Finally he spoke. "I shot him. With a .45 automatic." He looked up at the doctor. "In the side."

"You mean during the mass?"

"No, a couple of hours before that. Behind the mortuary—that's where I killed him."

"So he was dead? On the altar?"

"Yeah. Moving around like that." Paxton slowly shook his head, disbelieving his own words even as he said them. The fear he felt spreading across his face wasn't over the rat. It was for his sanity. "What does it mean?"

"You know it couldn't happen like that, don't you?"

Paxton nodded.

For a moment or two, the doctor toyed with the small malachite obelisk he used as a paperweight. Finally, he asked, "Is the rat in here now?"

Paxton answered at once. "No! He's in here," and he slapped his hand against his stomach. "He'll always be in here. He's mine now."

The doctor leaned forward, both his hands flat on the desk. "How did that happen?"

"He hid out in Padre's chalice during the mass. So I took the wine first, and drank it down. All of it." Paxton's face showed a triumphant little smile. "Now I've got him."

"You've got him?"

Paxton nodded with satisfaction. "And he's not getting out."

"Why?"

"Because when he's loose, he lives off soldiers' blood." His eyes glinted with anger. "Desecrates their bodies."

"Doesn't he try to get out?"

"Yes," he said grimly.

"Painful?"

"Yes."

"Right now?"

"Yes."

The doctor scrawled a few notes in the file in front of him, then leaned back in his chair, thinking. At last he said, "Is there anything else you've been seeing or hearing that you think might not really be there?"

"Sometimes I think so, but I'm not sure."

"Like what?"

Paxton nodded his head toward the window. The breeze coming through was sharpening, and they could see an afternoon thunderhead gathering above distant hills. "Can you smell that?"

"What, the rain coming on? Sure."

Paxton allowed himself a discouraged little smile and shook his head. "Not the rain."

"What, then?"

His face began to look fearful again. "You don't smell it."

"What?" The doctor watched as Paxton turned back toward the window, his nostrils flaring. "Tell me."

His eyes dropped to the floor. "Death," he said.

The doctor looked intently at him. "You smell death?"

Paxton started to get annoyed. "Dead bodies, doctor. The way it smells around the mortuary when they're burning stuff over there."

"I see."

Paxton gave him an appraising look. "You don't smell it, do you?" The doctor shook his head. "It's not there, is it?"

"No."

They sat together in silence for almost half a minute. At last, Paxton said, "What does it mean?"

The doctor didn't answer right away. "Is there anything else you've seen that you think probably wasn't there?"

This time Paxton didn't answer right away. Finally, he said, "I woke up last night..." He stopped.

"Not sleeping well?"

"Sleeping terrible." He sat there again, saying nothing.

"Even with the meds?" Paxton nodded.

The doctor made a brief note in the file. Then he said, "So when you woke up last night, you saw something?"

Paxton stirred, and nodded. "At the foot of the bed—it was Matt Kessler, just looking at me."

"Kessler?"

Paxton's face twisted with anguish. "The guy who was standing between me and the claymore when it went off. He took it all, and I didn't even get scratched."

"Did he blame you?"

"No, he'd never do that. But he looked like—like he still hadn't figured out what happened yet, what was going on with him." Paxton's voice changed as he acted like he was breaking bad news to Kessler. "Hey, Matt, you dumb shit—you're dead, man." The bitter half-grin he had forced ebbed away as he went on. "Lay down, why don't you?" His voice flattened and his eyes went glassy as they focused on the green obelisk paperweight. "Lay down." His words dulled out to an emotionless monotone.

Someone rapped twice on the door and opened it without waiting for a 'come in.' At once, the rain squall's wind pushed its way through the window and raced out the now open door. It sped across the desk and launched every loose piece of paper into the air. Doctor Brinker and Paxton simultaneously lunged for the sheets, manic in the wind, just as the office door slammed with a bang that shook the wall. At the sound, Paxton let out a cry of sheer terror and sank to his knees, grabbing hold of the edge of the desk.

Doctor Brinker was by his side in a second. He helped him stand and guided him back to his chair. He checked Paxton's pulse, frowned, and looked over at the man who had caused it all by coming in uninvited—Doctor Clarke, the colonel who commanded the psychiatric unit.

"Sorry about that," Clarke said. The two M.D.s gathered up the scattered papers while Paxton's color slowly returned.

Doctor Brinker closed the window, went to the door and called for an orderly to help Paxton back to his room. When they were gone, he turned to his boss, unapologetically angry.

"If that's you, this must be Thursday. Just come back from your regular chewing out by the MACV medical officer?" He sat down on one of the two easy chairs in the office, leaving the desk empty.

Clarke matched the anger. "I just caught hell over there for those three GIs you sent home last week, Brinker. You know the chain of command wants maximum return to units."

"Well, you're going to catch some more hell over the soldier you just sent to the moon with that door slam."

"What? God damn it... "

"Would you like to hear his symptoms before you send him back into combat?"

Clarke, his lips tightly pursed, sat down in the other easy chair. "Sure, why not?" he said.

"He's hallucinating rats and dead buddies, he's operating on the illusion that he's got the rat trapped inside himself, and you just saw his startle response. Caused it, in fact."

"You can't keep sending these people home before their tours are up."

"If Sergeant Paxton goes back to his unit now, he's going to get people killed. Simple as that. Is that what the chain of command wants?"

"Major, I want you to send this man back to his company."

"Colonel, if I don't, are you going to ship me home before *my* tour is up?"

"Why don't I just reassign you to morning sick call?"

Doctor Brinker gave a short laugh at that. "Ah, the kick-him-downstairs option." Then his voice grew deadly serious. "Do that, Colonel Clarke, and I'll poison every professional well you drink at, military and medical. I know how, and you know I know."

"You son of a bitch."

"Rock and a hard place, Colonel?"

This time, the slamming door shook the wall without the help of the wind.

HOME

CHAPTER 5

The home-team crowd roared approval when the football split the uprights. The cheerleaders leaped and twisted, and started a chant that the rowdy, half-filled stands picked up. The home-team Cougars were now up by two points on the Bushwackers. With only three minutes to play, all they had to do was knock down the inevitable flurry of desperation passes that were bound to come, and Paxton's old high school would come out winners.

He felt like he was more observing the crowd than being a part of it. Everyone else was on their feet, while he lolled back on his elbows in the next-to-last row of the wooden bleachers. He'd deliberately taken the high seat on the 20-yard line to avoid the people clustered below on the 50, and he'd spent much of the game idly checking the crowd to see who he recognized.

He was still puzzled by the young woman sitting two rows down from him and a bit closer to the midfield stripe with her son, who looked to be about three or so. She'd arrived late and slowly mounted the stands with the boy while he climbed the steps with his short legs. Paxton was sure he knew her from his student days. But she hadn't been in his class and he couldn't quite come up with her name.

Paxton had returned to Joachim Hill a little less than two weeks before and, although it was a jarring change that left him out of balance, he'd gotten himself a job at the local grocery right away—he knew he had to do something with his days.

During halftime, he could hear the boy asking his mom to get him a soda, while she kept resisting. Paxton thought she probably didn't want to fight the crowd. He was about to offer to get the boy a Coke when Brock Hermann, one of Paxton's old classmates, staggered up the steps and started talking to her. Judging from the way he took the steps, he'd had a few before he came and, despite the ban on alcohol, a few more since he got there. The young mother's face wrinkled involuntarily as he leaned in and started talking. He must have reeked. When he clumsily put his hand on her shoulder, she stood up, indignant, and ripped into him verbally for a few seconds. Paxton caught a bit of it, something about getting one of the cops down at the foot of the bleachers.

Brock had always been a pain to be around, always full of himself. His dad owned the Chevy dealership and Brock had gotten a brand new convertible for his sixteenth birthday, a Chevelle SS396—which gave him an enormous edge with the girls. Paxton knew daddy had brought him into the company after college, with the result that Brock had too much money and too much time. And it looked like too much booze. He wore a baseball cap with 'Joachim Hill Motors' sewn across an outline of the state of Missouri. Some day he'd likely own the dealership, but right now Paxton guessed Joachim Hill Motors owned Brock. At last he reeled back down the bleachers.

Suddenly, with a minute and thirty seconds left, one of the Cougars intercepted a Bushwacker pass and fell on it. The crowd was on its feet again, roaring. Now all the Cougars had to do was run out the clock. The cheerleaders went airborne again, all pompoms and whirling hair. And that's when Paxton realized who the young mother was. Ellen LaSoeur had been a cheerleader herself and although she was in the class behind his own, she'd always caught his eye at the Friday night games.

As the Bushwackers were delaying the inevitable by using their last time out, Brock headed back up the bleachers again, looking equally contrite and befuddled. If she'd been by herself, Ellen could have avoided him easily, but she had to shepherd the boy. As Brock reached her, Paxton stood and made his way down to her. Indignant and just a little afraid, she was talking to Brock.

"Will you *please* leave me alone," she said.

"Ellen, now don't be mad—I just want to help you with Todd," and he looked hazily at her son.

"Hey, Brock," Paxton said. "What's up?"

"What?" Brock refocused on Paxton with difficulty. "Oh, hi, Chuck. I'm just helping Ellen here," and he put his hand clumsily on her shoulder. She shrugged it off at once.

"Brock, I swear..." She swept Todd up in her arms, grabbed her tote bag, and started walking away from Brock toward the other stairs.

"Now don't be like that, Ellen..." As Brock started to follow her, Paxton grabbed his baseball cap. Brock felt the top of his head and turned to Paxton. "Damn it, Chuck."

"Nice hat," Paxton said, looking at the logo.

"Give it back."

Paxton strode up the three rows to the top of the bleachers. "Come and get it," he said, and grinned.

"Shit," Brock said in a kind of exasperated mumble, and started climbing. He reached the top and put a hand on the guardrail to steady himself. "Now give it here."

Paxton tossed Brock's cap off the back of the bleachers and watched it land on the roof of a little lean-to shed where the athletic department kept lawn mowers and line-marking equipment.

"Your grandmother really shouldn't have let you come out tonight," Brock said.

Paxton felt the color rising in his face. "You used to say that a lot to me when we were in high school. I didn't like it then, either."

"Well, tough," Brock answered. "You jock guys were all a pain in the ass. And *you* still are," he added, slurring his words. He bent down under the guardrail to see where the hat had landed. At that moment, the game ended and the crowd broke into boisterous cheers. Paxton pivoted around to look at the field in a way that put his hips up against Brock's rear, and thrust sharply backwards. Nobody heard Brock's yell above the cheering, or the sound he made hitting the roof of the shed. Paxton glanced over the edge of the bleachers. One of the side walls of the shed had collapsed and the roof had slid completely off, Brock riding it to the ground. He lay on his back in the rubble looking stunned, but began stirring a bit.

Paxton easily caught up with Ellen in the crowd.

"Hey, Ellen."

She turned apprehensively, but saw it was Paxton and relaxed.

"You okay?" he asked.

"I think so," she answered. "Where's Brock?"

"He went out the other way. He was kind of disoriented, wasn't he?"

"He always seemed to find his way back to me real easy."

Paxton chuckled. "Yeah, he did that all right." They were out of the bleachers now, heading for the parking lot. "Can I carry Todd for you? He looks like he's getting pretty big."

"Is he ever," she laughed. "I'd appreciate it. Honey," she said to her son, "Chuck's going to carry you to the car now, okay?"

"Will we go to the Top Hat?" he asked. He was obviously up past his bedtime, but the possibility of going to one of the local eateries began to energize him.

"Why don't we grab a bite?" Paxton asked.

Ellen smiled. "Oh, I suppose so," she said.

Paxton carried Todd to Ellen's car and then followed her to the Top Hat. They recognized several people there from the game, and the home team win had the restaurant crowd in a good mood.

"Hi, Judy," Ellen said to one of the waitresses. "Have you got a booth?"

"Let me clear that one over there," the waitress said. "Starting to get busy after the game."

Ellen slid into one side of the booth and began passing glasses and plates to the waitress. Todd slipped his hand into Paxton's while they waited. Paxton looked down at the boy, who was watching the two women clearing the table, and smiled.

When the table was ready, Todd joined Ellen on her side of the booth. She made sure he was on the inside to keep him from roaming around. As Paxton slid into the opposite side, the waitress brought a booster seat and took their order. Ellen and Paxton went for burgers and Cokes. All Todd wanted was french fries with lots of ketchup. They added a small orange juice.

When Ellen tried to get Todd settled on the booster seat, the boy said, "Mommy, I'm big now. I don't need that."

"You're probably going to need it when the food comes," she said. "You don't want to get ketchup all over your shirt."

"Let's see if you need it when your fries get here," Paxton told him.

"Okay," the boy said. Ellen started to relax.

"I really appreciate you distracting Brock back there so we could make our getaway," she said to Paxton. "He drinks way too much."

"Well, it looked like the fair lady was in a bit of distress there," he replied with a smile. "I don't think he's real happy being his dad's heir apparent." He tried to glance unobtrusively at her empty ring finger, but she noticed anyway. He wondered if she'd been expecting it.

"I took back my maiden name after the divorce," she said, answering the question he hadn't asked.

"I'm sorry," Paxton replied. "It's just I was curious about..." He finished the sentence with a shrug.

"Oh, I know," she responded. "Sometimes I can't believe everything that's happened in the past five years."

That took Paxton by surprise. "It's not...has it been that long already?"

"Has it ever."

For a fraction of a second Paxton felt that his life before Nam had happened to somebody else, that now *he* was somebody else. He shook it off. "Who was the lucky groom?" he asked. Todd slid off the bench more or less unnoticed and ducked under the table.

She poked her straw into her Coke once or twice and smiled a little. "Brock's the proud daddy," she said.

"Oh, man." Paxton was clearly surprised. "I hope he's all right." Ellen looked puzzled. "I mean, I hope he makes it home okay. He was pretty far gone. But he shouldn't have mentioned my grandmother like that." Todd's head poked up on Paxton's side of the table. He rumpled the boy's hair.

"Your grandmother?"

"Yeah. You probably don't remember, but my mom died when I was about Todd's age, maybe a little younger. So dad got his mom, my grandmother, to move in and take care of me. She'd been widowed for a couple of years already."

"Oh, wait. Marge Paxton—she used to play bingo with my own grandmother over at St. Brendan's." Todd ducked back under the table. Ellen's hand shot out and got a grip on his shirt, but he shook loose and stayed out of reach. "Those two were bingo buddies, all right. So Marge Paxton's your grandmother?"

"I always just call her Nana."

A thought struck Ellen. "Oh, boy. Sometimes when the booze talks—I mean, Brock didn't say anything..."

"In bad taste?"

She nodded, looking relieved that he'd filled in the gap for her. Todd's head slowly emerged on Paxton's side again, just enough so he could keep tabs on his mother.

"No," Paxton answered, "but he said something that the guys back in school would say when they wanted to get me mad. 'Your grandmother shouldn't have let you out.' Trying to push my buttons."

"The booze talked like that a lot when we were married."

"He's pretty young to be this far gone. Was he that way when you married him?"

"Oh, yes. In fact, alcohol's basically how it all happened," she said. "We got drunk, I got pregnant, we got married, I sued for divorce. All in 18 months." Todd was struggling to get up on Paxton's bench.

"Here you go, Todd," and Paxton lifted him up and sat him on his lap.

The boy smiled happily. "You're my booster seat, okay?"

Paxton smiled back. "Deal."

"It was that damned convertible," she continued. "Lipstick red."

"I hope you got a good settlement."

She shook her head. "Brock's dad hired a lawyer from Saint Louis. He didn't want any green hemorrhages bleeding out the family fortune." She shrugged. "I get something for Todd's upkeep, and it helps. But I still have to wait tables over at Herb's. Morning shift—early." The waitress brought their food.

"How early do you go in?" Paxton took charge of the ketchup bottle for Todd.

"Get there by 5:30, and set up for the 6 a.m. breakfast boys."

"Ouch." He glanced at his watch and gave a little frown.

"And you know how the men in this town are. Once you're divorced, you're *really* fair game." Her voice changed to mock indignation as she said, "That's *not* the table leg you've got ahold of there, Pard."

Paxton chuckled. "Does Brock get to visit Todd?"

"Oh, yes," she said. "And take him over to grandpa. Three generations of Hermann boys."

"So you kept your daddy's name?" he asked Todd. The boy nodded his head as he licked ketchup off one of the french fries. "And money can't buy happiness, right?"

She smiled ruefully. "All right, that's enough out of me," she said. "More than enough. What've you been up to since you left?"

"Oh, well..." He realized instinctively there were things he didn't want to tell her, but for the life of him, he couldn't think of what they might be. Maybe not events, maybe feelings. He continued very carefully, while struggling to sound casual. "After graduation, I hung around here for six months or so. Doing odd jobs, waiting for my draft notice. I finally got tired of life on hold and enlisted."

"You went in for three years."

"The basic enlistment was three years. But after I got in, I volunteered for airborne training, and that put some more time on top." He didn't tell her how much and left out the months he spent in a stateside Army hospital after they evacuated him from Nam.

"So how was it?" She asked. "Vietnam, I mean."

The question instantly triggered an uncontrolled montage of memories: choppers coming in at their base camp to take them out on another mission. A leech firmly attached to his calf. Yelling desperately into his radio to get artillery support under heavy enemy fire. Kessler at the mortuary, the inside of his half-empty skull thick with ants. The rat on the makeshift altar, staring at him with its intense red eyes. Paxton's stomach churned.

"Chuck?" Her lips were parted, and a worried crease had appeared between her eyebrows.

He jerked his head up as if he'd caught himself falling asleep while driving. "Well, you know." He tried to smile reassuringly, but it didn't come out right. "It was just something I had to get through."

She put a hand on his for a moment. "I read you were wounded," she said.

"Yeah." He looked down at his burger. "Twice, actually." He glanced up at her, shrugged, and looked away again.

"Were you shot?" Her face showed concern and curiosity in equal parts. She didn't realize what this line of questioning was doing to him.

"Ellen..." The conversation was making him more and more anguished. "I...I don't like to go back there." She was frankly puzzled. "Up here, I mean," he added. He could feel the pained expression on his face and tried to get rid of it.

"Oh, Chuck." At last she realized the impact her questions were having on him. "Oh, I'm so sorry." Her hand went back to his arm. He forced a smile.

"Don't worry about it. Really. It's already a lot better than it was." True as far as it went, but also a lie of omission.

"I'm full, Mommy," Todd said. Paxton, grateful for the interruption, dipped the corner of a paper napkin into a glass of water and started working on the boy's hands and face. "Let's get you cleaned up," he told him.

"Chuck's not done with his burger yet."

"Oh, I think I've had enough." He caught the eye of the waitress and got the check. He was glad he'd gotten paid that day.

On the way out, he carried Todd. The boy pillowed his head on Paxton's shoulder. When they got to Ellen's car, she said, "Let's not be strangers, all right?"

"Sounds good to me," he replied.

"Sunday and Monday are my days off," she told him.

"I've got a regular weekend, Saturday and Sunday." She opened the rear door of her car, and Paxton laid the boy on the back seat. He was almost asleep.

"Good," she said. "At least we'll have a bit of an overlap. Let's do something this Sunday."

"I'll call you," he promised.

He did, and the three of them went to a matinee of *Bullitt*. When the car chase started, Todd climbed up on Paxton's lap. Ellen was wide-eyed, not quite believing what she was seeing. The other two were fascinated. When Steve McQueen's Mustang went airborne in one quick cut, Paxton exclaimed, "Look at that!"

"Yeah!" Todd answered. He was taking his cues from Paxton on how to react to the movie.

Afterward, they went to Ellen's apartment for a supper of soup and sandwiches. She told Paxton that Brock had dislocated his shoulder and cut his face and neck falling backwards off the stands. He couldn't remember what happened, but when she and Todd visited him in the hospital, Brock's father was already there and he was really angry. He told Brock he'd better get a grip on his drinking and told Ellen frankly that he was beginning to understand why she'd divorced him after 18 months. Later, after dinner when she saw him out, Paxton put a quick kiss on her lips. She smiled and said, "See you."

⚹

Next day, Paxton and the grocery store manager parted company. Looking back on it, Paxton knew it shouldn't have happened. While he was restocking canned goods, he got deep into remembering Captain Bonner and 'send your best squad leader,' and how it had led straight to Kessler's death. He couldn't get rid of a mental picture of Kessler's mutilated skull. In a way he was glad, because the intensifying hatred of Bonner generated a malicious kind of pleasure.

That was when the manager came by. "Hey, Chuck," he said. "Put the perishable dairy stuff in the refrigerator cases first, and then do the canned goods."

Paxton looked at him with all the loathing he felt at that moment for Bonner. "Fuck you," he said, and started taking off his apron.

The manager was astonished. "What?"

Paxton balled up the apron and threw it on the floor. "Fuck you!" And he strode out of the market.

At the end of the week, the mail brought Paxton a check for the four hours of work he'd clocked that Monday, with 'terminated' in the remarks block.

✴

"Butt first, Nana." Paxton was holding his grandmother's walker steady as she backed into the passenger seat of his car. Once she was firmly seated, she swung her legs in. It was a chilly Sunday afternoon even by December standards, but it was near the first anniversary of his father's death, and he and Nana decided to visit the cemetery.

Once she was settled, she repeated his instruction: "Butt first. Butt first. Your father always said the same thing."

"That's where I learned it," Paxton smiled. He closed her door, folded up her walker and put it in the trunk. "I told Ellen we'd pick her and Todd up about two," he said as he started up the car. "We'll probably make him miss his nap, but he's usually a pretty good little kid."

"Another Hermann boy. That family's got entirely too much money."

"Todd doesn't."

"No, but he will. Wait till it comes time for college, grandpa will step right in."

Nana held three bouquets of plastic flowers on her lap. Now and then she would pick at a petal as they rode along in silence. When they reached Ellen's apartment building, she and Todd were just coming out. Paxton held the back door open for the two of them as they climbed in.

"Hi, Mrs. Paxton," Ellen said as she settled Todd beside her.

"Call me Nana, Ellen."

She noticed the bouquets Nana was holding. "I brought some flowers, too. For my grandmother's grave. She's not far from the Paxton plot," Ellen said.

"I dearly loved that woman," Nana said. "We played bingo together for over thirty years. She picked me up every week after I had to start using the walker. I always say I didn't lose my bingo buddy, I lost my ride." She gave a little laugh, and then sighed. "Oh, I do miss that lady."

When Nana insisted on walking the short distance to the graves, Paxton got the walker out of the trunk and held her arm as they picked their way across the dried brown grass. Ellen carried Nana's flowers along with her own. Todd was wide-eyed, and Paxton wondered if he'd ever been to a cemetery before.

"Put one of those bouquets by your grandpa's marker," Nana told Paxton. He did, and they all stood there in silence for a moment at her husband's grave.

"I miss you too, Percy," she said finally. "Percy," she repeated. "Who'd name their son Percival, anyway?" She shook her head. "Put those other two on your mom and dad's graves." He did, lingering by his father's headstone.

Nana broke the quiet as she looked at her son's grave. "Parents should never have to bury their children," she said. "Ellen, take us to your grandma's grave."

Nana kept their pace slow. When Ellen set her own flowers on the grave, the older woman said an Our Father, a Hail Mary and a Glory Be. "May they rest in peace," she added at the end.

From the cemetery they went back to Ellen's apartment for

Sunday dinner. While Ellen prepared the chuck roast, and the carrots and potatoes, Nana sat at the kitchen table so they could talk. From there Nana could see Paxton sitting on the floor in front of the television. His crossed legs made the perfect seat for Todd. He rested his hands across the stomach of the boy, who was leaning back against Paxton's chest.

"Look at those two," she said to Ellen. "Fit together pretty well, don't they?"

Ellen looked up at the two in the living room and smiled. "They do," she said, then added, "Gravy's ready. I'm going to put it on."

On the way home from Ellen's, Nana broke the silence. "Did Ellen get an annulment from the Church?" she asked.

"Where did that come from?" Paxton responded.

"I was just wondering. In case she wants to get married again by a priest."

"I don't know," he said. He paused a moment and then added rather pointedly, "It's never come up."

"I was just wondering," she repeated, and lapsed back into silence.

As they pulled up at the house and he set the brake, she said, "If you married her, you could adopt Todd and make him a Paxton, you know."

"Nana, that's really enough now."

"All right, all right."

Paxton helped her into the house and got her settled, then told her he was going back to Ellen's for a little while. Nana said nothing, not even next morning when he returned. In a few weeks, he moved in with Ellen and Todd, making sure that Nana always had her groceries and meals and got to her medical appointments, and seeing that her walk was shoveled when Joachim Hill got snow.

In January, Paxton started working at Old Man Deutsch's garage, repairing cars. By the end of the winter he was unemployed again. Ellen tried to be patient. She sensed that his work problems at the supermarket and the garage were related somehow to what he'd gone through in the war, but she was clueless about the exact nature of the connection. In any case, he was usually a considerate lover—and at least his kisses didn't taste like Brock's bourbon and stale cigarettes.

CHAPTER 6

"**D**amn it, Chuck. Cut your grandma's grass."

For the third time, Ellen breathed the command toward his ear from where her head was pillowed on his shoulder. She was determined not to wake Todd in the next room. Paxton's sleepy grunt could have meant yes, no, or I'll think about it.

She raised her head. "Did you hear me?"

They lay naked against each other on her bed, her arm across his chest and her thigh nestled gently between his legs. His own thigh was returning the favor. He'd made a long night of it for them. If once isn't enough, she wondered, and twice is too much, what's three times? Depends on whether you have to go to work in the morning. He didn't. He'd lost another job last week, this time at the Quick Shop. But Ellen did—up at five as usual, in to Herb's to set up and wait on tables right through lunch. She'd finish the cleanup by about 2:30 or so and be out of there. At least when Paxton was between jobs, she didn't have to take her son over to her sister's house at the crack of dawn. Paxton would do the day care bit, and quite well—but she'd still be glad when Todd started preschool in the fall.

Paxton had been back from Vietnam nearly six months already. They'd been an item almost the whole time, and she gradually came to realize there were some nights when his sleep wouldn't rest him if he hadn't literally screwed himself into oblivion. It was not all that often, thank goodness, but every now and then. A few times, she called a halt after a double, and his sleep had been restless and troubled. Once, she shut them down after a single, pleading sweetly, she hoped, the lateness of the hour. She woke in the night, frightened from his grip on her arm. He was kneeling upright on the bed, naked and dripping with sweat, staring wide-eyed at something she couldn't see. His breathing soughed eerily in the dark of the still room. Even now, she was convinced he'd been asleep, kneeling there with his eyes wide open.

When she prodded, he told her of being in a vast room, walls invisible in the surrounding blackness, trapped inside a cell of light. Saffron-robed Orientals at altars of chrome glided noiselessly, floating straight toward him, as if to do him harm. They came at him from every direction. He couldn't stand still, but always had to be dodging them, jumping out of their way. He didn't answer her question about what was on the altars, and declined the offer she wrapped inside a long, gentle kiss. When the alarm woke her early the next morning, he was still staring at the ceiling. After that, she never said no— no matter how tired she was.

"Did you *hear* me?" she repeated, raising up on her left elbow and shifting herself directly above him.

"You're mashin' my danglies, darlin'," he drawled. He extricated them from between their thighs. With his finger, he began tracing gentle circles around the nipple hanging above his face.

"Chuck..."

"All right, don't wake the boy now. I'll do the grass tomorrow afternoon, when you get back."

✹

102

When she arrived home, they were following a Bugs Bunny cartoon with rapt attention. He lay belly down in his jeans, shirtless and barefoot on the living room floor. Todd was sitting astride his buttocks, with a little stack of flower-shaped butter cookies nestled in the small of his back. They would laugh simultaneously whenever the Bunny gave Yosemite Sam his comeuppance. There was a part of Paxton, she had long since decided, that needed to start preschool with Todd in September, and she grudgingly admitted it was part of what made him attractive to her.

She waited till cartoons were done and cajoled him out the door. Todd still took a piece of a nap most afternoons, thank God, which meant she could catch 40 winks herself.

Paxton pulled up at Nana's house, calling his car names no sailor ever heard. But it was behaving the way any car would, given how he maintained it. He knew he should replace the points, clean the plugs, and reset the gaps again, and he was overdue for an oil change. When he finally added a quart two weeks ago, Old Man Deutsch had asked him tartly if he was trying to wean it. They were back on speaking terms again after Paxton quit, but he could sense the old man keeping his distance—no 'how's Ellen,' no 'Nana doing all right?' No small talk at all.

Paxton suspected his car had a slow oil leak, probably at the drain plug. He'd taken a pint of some kind of sludge-out from the shelves of the convenience store where he worked and poured it into his gas tank after neglecting to pay for it. The owner, Mrs. Hutchinson, fired him rather than having him arrested, as she usually did in such cases. With his combat record, she complained, they wouldn't jail him for committing an axe murder on live TV.

She was probably right. He found when he got back to Joachim Hill that he'd become a big deal in the little town. While he was in-country, his grandmother had clipped all pertinent articles out of the paper and gradually accumulated a scrapbook. The commander of the helicopter unit had put him in for a Distinguished Service Cross for his last action, but it had been downgraded to a Silver Star. A local editorial decried the downgrading, and Congressman Hemmings was quoted two days in a row ranting about how he would deal with the Defense budget to exact retribution—which in the middle of a war, Paxton knew, was ridiculous on its face. After getting some mileage out of a small-town war hero, the congressman duly subsided.

Paxton, standing by his car, looked up at the house. His parents had bought the three-bedroom place when they got married. His dad told him once they'd wanted to have a couple more kids. But when Paxton was two, his mother had been killed outright on a two-lane highway in one of those horrendous collisions with a tractor-trailer. Paxton's widowed grandmother agreed to move in and take care of him. She still lived there.

He knew she was sitting in the faded maroon armchair watching him. She would wait patiently because she couldn't take more than a few steps without her walker and she hated having to use it.

His gaze shifted to the porch. The screening in the lower half of the door needed replacing. It had been pretty well shredded by the clawing of his dog, Pistol, and the animal had been dead two years already. But with Pistol in the ground in the backyard, the ripped screen was about all that testified to his having been there. The porch floor caught his eye, and again he told himself he needed to put a couple of coats of gray deck paint on it before next winter. Otherwise, the planks would start to rot and get dangerous. As it was, his grandmother was beginning to snag a leg of her walker in the little crannies that were starting to show up.

Then, as he always did when he came home, he pictured his father on the porch as he'd stood there the day Paxton left for Vietnam. Tissue in hand, his grandmother had hung back in the house, so when Paxton turned to wave a last good-bye, his father stood there alone. In the moment it took him to raise his arm and wave, it had finally struck Paxton that he really might not get back, that this moment, right now, might be the last time they would ever see each other again. It was only on the flight back for his father's funeral six months into his tour that he recollected their farewell from the older man's perspective. His father had known how far advanced his cancer was, while Paxton hadn't the faintest idea it was even there. Why hadn't he told him? "He didn't want it preying on your mind," Nana said. "He was afraid it would make you careless."

So he'd stood saluting at the side of his father's grave while the nation acknowledged his World War II service with the triple volley and taps. Paxton already wore his first Bronze Star and Purple Heart on his uniform, but that didn't seem important as his father was given his final salute. That night, Paxton had been oppressed, realizing he must soon leave this place of the dead to go back to that other. On his return flight he felt the presence of death pervading sky and sea, and when he looked, no land was visible in any direction.

He absently patted the fender of his car and started up the cracked concrete walk.

The grass stood almost a foot high. The unusually heavy rains, combined with the growing warmth of spring, left it thick and lush. The mowing would take him longer than he planned, and there might not be enough gas in the can they kept out back in the shed. Ought to have Ferd Antrim bring his goats over—charge to graze 'em. He smiled and went in.

"That you, Chuck?" He knew she'd watched him pull up and make his slow way along the walk.

"Yeah, Nana. Thought I'd cut the grass." He'd already told her that on the phone.

"Sure does need it." The nasal flatness of her voice was tinged ever so lightly with complaint. Her hair was neater, he noted, than when he came by unannounced. Her walker stood at hand beside the chair, but while he was in the house he would be her feet.

"Pot's on the stove," she said.

"Sounds good." He went into the kitchen and lit the gas under the old percolator. While the morning's coffee heated, he got two cups from the cupboard and put a couple of teaspoons of sugar in one, along with a dollop of milk out of the carton. He raised his voice. "Want a cup?"

"Why, I think I just might," she answered, "though I'll have to hobble to the bathroom right after." She laughed that little laugh of hers, full yet shy, and added an afterthought. "I think *two* spoons of sugar today."

He poured the coffee, swished a spoon through hers a few times, and took it in.

"You ought to take your coffee with milk and a little sugar, Chuck. Always drink it black and bitter like that, it'll make your stomach get achy."

"I'd rather have it plain, Nana." He grinned. "Don't want my coffee sweeter than Ellen." As a child, he'd learned to be charming to keep the conversation from getting too picky.

"You ought to marry that girl." Sometimes, charm didn't work. "I'm sure she wants to, to put up with you like she does. And I swear young Todd must think you're his daddy, or wish you was."

"I'm not ready for something that permanent yet." He was getting uncomfortable.

"Jess Scroggins has a job open at the hardware store, Chuck." He decided that 'permanent' had reminded her of his employment record lately. The subtleties beneath the plain flatness of her voice always amazed him. Right now, he was hearing concern, even anxiety. Her change of subject made him feel bad that he'd been fired again, but he knew that wasn't her purpose. "Nettie called to tell me," she went on, "and she said he wouldn't advertise it in the paper till the weekend. You could get it before most people know it's out there."

"Maybe I'll swing by after I finish the grass." He knew the lawn would keep him past the store's closing time.

"Don't go over there all sweaty. See him first thing in the morning."

"That's a good idea."

They talked while the coffee lasted. He said he'd shop for some groceries for her when he finished the grass and went outside.

The weathered little house sat on a big lot bounded by old oaks and sycamores. For as long as he could remember, his father had scattered the lawn cuttings under half-a-dozen trees growing tightly together in the back left corner by the street. Stray cats would rove through to hunt the voles that nested there. Back in the days of the push mower, his father would rake up the fresh cuttings, walk them over to the grove, and toss them loose into the air. When Paxton was twelve, they bought the power mower Paxton still used, emptying the catch bag under the trees as often as it filled. They'd been using this mower, he realized, for half his life.

Today, the catch bag filled frequently. He had to push the mower slowly through the thick grass to keep it from stalling. Clumps of the cuttings would clog the mouth of the bag before it was full. As he put the last of the gas in the mower, he knew the fuel would give out before the grass did.

He'd been sweating freely for almost an hour when he found himself reaching absently for the canteen he hadn't worn in a good many months. He smiled a tight little smile. After drinking two brimming glasses of water standing at the kitchen sink, he helped his grandmother move with her walker to the back porch and onto the battered rocker so she could watch him work. He draped his T-shirt over the railing and mentally noted that he'd forgotten to take his salt pills with the water, which would tick off their cadre NCO; but now the army had decided it was better after all not to take so much salt in pill form. Hard on the heels of that realization, he remembered again that he wasn't in the army any more and hadn't been for some time.

He gave his head a little shake to clear the cobwebs. Every now and again, he found that his mind's eye was looking out from his old uniform. At first, it amused him until it dawned on him that it was somehow linked to wherever those dreams came from. He decided that the profuse sweating and the green quiet, broken by the noise of the mower, must be taking him back to the Vietnam Delta. But where were those dreams coming from? He gave the pull cord a jerk, and the engine caught.

One time, when he had the mower on its side to scrape out hunks of drying grass, he'd been struck by how its blade was a miniature copy of a helicopter's main rotor. A 30-inch length of steel a couple of inches across, it was bolted exactly at its midpoint to the engine shaft, its blades canted to efficiently sweep the grass. As the mower's engine settled into its idle speed, he felt distinctly uneasy knowing the blade was spinning beneath the chassis—not because it could harm but because, despite reasoning coolly with himself, it continued to remind him of the Hueys he used to ride into combat, the memories, and especially the feelings. Standing there staring at the beat-up mower, he felt his stomach flutter with fear at the day's mission, while his mind kept telling him he wasn't going anywhere.

He tried to remind himself that this green was grass, not bamboo or nipa palm. This was lawn. This was home. He deliberately whiffed the mower's exhaust, so different from the fumes of a Huey's combusted JP-4, and contrasted the start-up sequences of the two machines. A pull on the cord and in seconds the mower idled at speed, but a Huey's rotor sometimes took almost a minute sucking power from the nickel-cadmium battery before the engine could sustain itself. The two were totally different. His pulse began to slow and his breaths lengthen. He smiled at his grandmother on the porch, tossed his head as if to say 'here we go,' and began the first pass in the back yard.

He settled into a slow, steady pace, moving at right angles to the house. He'd been stupid not to pay for the gasoline additive at the convenience store, which cost no more than a handful of change. The motor strained and slowed, and he eased his pace for a few steps. He clearly remembered that day's logic, how his pay from Mrs. Hutchinson was much too low and the cost of the additive would contribute a bit to righting that wrong. True but irrelevant. Stealing was stealing, and she'd fired him on the spot. With a *thunk* the mower picked up a marble-sized stone, hurled it out from under the chassis, and bounced it off the toe of his old combat boot. If it had hit a few inches higher, it would have stung sharply. Sometimes, when an NVA mortar round went off close by, secondary fragments—the pieces of junk scooped up and flung about by the force of the explosion—could do more damage than the primary fragments. It depended on their speed, the sharpness of their edges and the angle of impact.

He reached the porch steps at the top of the hill and swung the mower back around. The most effective fragments he'd ever seen were the fléchettes of a howitzer's beehive round. One night, when Paxton's platoon was pulling security for an artillery fire support base, they came under heavy ground attack—from a reinforced battalion, the intel guys told them when it was all over. He guided the mower down the slope toward the back fence and the creek beyond. Most of the perimeter was well dug in with concertina and mines. They were holding their own with their defensive fires and getting supporting artillery from neighboring bases. The mower reached the fence, and Paxton swung it back uphill—he'd probably make it all the way to the porch steps again before he needed to empty the bag. The fire base was most vulnerable where the road entered the perimeter. In the light of illuminating flares, they could see a determined element of NVA fighting their way up the dirt track by sheer discipline and desperation, hemmed in to the roadbed as they were by tangles of barbed wire and thickly sown mines on either side. Judging by the satchel charges several of them carried, they were sappers, with a large contingent of supporting infantry. They were bent on blowing open a gap in the perimeter. They were taking casualties but still had a good chance of actually pulling it off. Paxton hit a stretch of lawn that was shaded all day, and the grass, though tall, was not as thick. He picked up speed just a bit. The fire base commander, a young artillery captain, ordered one of his howitzers to sight straight down the road, the barrel parallel to the ground in direct lay. Back in the full sun, the grass thickened again and slowed him, but he knew he'd make it to the top before the catch bag filled. On the captain's command, the howitzer fired the beehive round, sending a widening cone of thousands of steel fléchettes sweeping straight down the road, hacking out a trail of carnage and blood and torn bodies that was...

Suddenly, the mower's blade struck something, ringing with the sharp *krang* of a hammer striking sheet steel full force. The mower halted in place, its revs dipping low for a second, then recovered. At the same time fragments of something scattered out from beneath the mower, one of them striking Paxton sharply on his bare chest and leaving him gasping. His hand went instinctively to the spot and came away bloody.

"I'm hit!"

He looked at the grass by the mower and saw a fan-shaped scatter of blood and unrecognizable tissue. *Who else is wounded?* "Medic!" He doubled over and sank into a sitting position, the noise of the revving engine in his ears. Incredibly, his senses were telling him that he was hunched in a medivac chopper again, waiting for other wounded to be loaded aboard. The engine was pounding, and he could see the backs of the two pilots' helmets as they waited to take off. In a panic of fear and self-doubt, his mind clung desperately to its knowledge that the noise wasn't a Huey, that the fan of blood and flesh on the grass was a grotesque fantasy, that he only needed to reach up and cut the old mower's engine. But he sat helpless and afraid, paralyzed by the struggle between his mind and his senses.

At the sound of the impact and his cry, his grandmother stood. "Chuck?" When he didn't answer she called again: "Chuck!"

She was sure the mower had hit him with a piece of broken glass or a strand of wire and began laboriously to descend the steps with her walker. She cleared the stairs and started across the lawn toward him, but a leg of her walker tangled in the thick grass. As she lurched and fell, her mouth glanced off the walker and her lower lip began to bleed. The plush, matted lawn cushioned her fall somewhat, but she was half stunned. She moaned, called to Paxton once or twice and lay still.

For another two minutes, he huddled there immobile, while she lay quietly, not moving. At last, the engine began to stutter. It stalled, revived briefly, and diminished slowly to silence.

"Chuck," she called again, but he still didn't respond. The woman next door came out on her back porch, took one look, and hurried over.

"Chuck," she said, "help me with your grandmother." He looked at her without seeming to understand what was happening. She moved Nana to the porch steps by herself and called the police.

When the officer arrived, he got Paxton to his feet and sat him next to Nana on the steps.

"Anybody else hit?" Paxton asked, holding his chest.

"What?" the cop asked.

"Who else got hit?"

"Your grandmother's got a cut on her lip and maybe a sprained thumb, but she's okay."

"When are they going to get the medivac moving?"

"Medivac?"

"What are they waiting for?"

"They, uh—they'll be moving it out ASAP. I'm not sure what's holding it up." He looked toward the mower and saw the blood and flesh fanning out on the grass. He immediately looked at Paxton's boots, but they were in one piece. He turned back to the bloody grass. "Now, where'd that come from?"

Paxton followed his gaze and was surprised. "You can see it?"

The cop gave him a weird look. "Couldn't miss it." He walked over to the mower and pushed it forward a couple of feet. Underneath was a large box turtle, missing its entire upper section and revealing a bloody interior. The mower's blade had hacked off the top inch of its superstructure, fragmenting it and spewing it out from under the mower. He found that Paxton's hand clutched a piece of turtle shell and some of its blood, but the skin on his chest was hardly broken.

"We need to get your grandmother over to Doc Reineke and get her checked out. And he'll need to swab that cut on your chest with something to make sure it doesn't get infected."

Dr. Reineke, a rumpled man smelling of antiseptic and cigars, saw Nana first, pronounced her shaken but otherwise sound, and helped her to the waiting room. Next, he dealt with the small laceration on Paxton's chest. As Paxton pulled on his T-shirt, the doctor turned to him.

"Sit down, Chuck. We need to talk a minute."

Paxton's face at once became concerned. "Is she all right?"

"She's fine. It's you I'm worried about."

"Oh, I'm okay. Our medic Doc Watson would send me straight back to duty without even a Band-Aid."

Dr. Reineke pulled at one of his bushy eyebrows and looked at the man before him. He'd gone to Paxton's house right after the midwife delivered him, declaring both mother and son in good health. As time went on, he'd medicated Paxton's fevers and stitched up his cuts, but some hurts, he well knew, he was unqualified to treat.

"Do you think about Vietnam very much?"

"Oh...you know, off and on." The grin he forced didn't come out as charming as he wanted.

"Officer Daniels says you thought you were back over there." Tom—Officer Daniels—had been a senior when Paxton was a freshman at the county's consolidated high school. Referring to him in his official capacity made this quite a formal occasion.

"Well, that piece of shell hit real hard, and I saw the blood. It caught me by surprise, I guess."

"Did you...let's see now, how to put this. Did you know your head..." He tapped his temple. "...wasn't where your body was?"

Paxton paused, then nodded. As he remembered his feelings sitting by the mower, the old fear crept across his face. "I wanted to come back, but I couldn't. I couldn't shut it off."

Dr. Reineke pulled at his eyebrow again. "Ever have bad dreams?"

Paxton hesitated, but nodded again. He turned an apprehensive face to the older man. "What is it?"

"Nothing all that unusual. Every war gives it to some of the people who fight in it. In World War I, they called it shell shock. In your Dad's war, it was combat fatigue. Now, they're starting to give it a new name. Some people are calling it battle trauma."

"What does it mean?"

"Sometimes, after soldiers get home, they have nightmares. Or maybe there's trouble holding a job." Paxton's eyes dropped. "That's part of it sometimes. They can even have flashbacks to when they were over there. Something happens to trigger it—they're standing here at home in broad daylight, but it's like they're back in the war and they can't make it stop. Like today."

Paxton looked at him. "Can you do anything for it?"

"I don't know anybody in town who can, but there are people out there who know how to deal with it."

A flicker of hope crossed Paxton's face. "Where?"

"The VA just opened a storefront clinic for Vietnam vets in Saint Louis. They've got people on staff who spend the whole day working on just this. They're the ones you need to see."

Paxton recalled the fan-shaped smear of blood on the grass, which he thought was a figment but turned out to be real. It was like the smell of death at the Tan Son Nhut mortuary that day, which also ended up being real when he'd have sworn it was his imagination. The rat at Padre's mass had seemed the real thing to him until it veered to show the hole in its side. Reluctantly, he concluded that he couldn't always tell what was inside his head any more and what was outside. Dr. Reineke made an appointment for him in Saint Louis the next day.

✖

"No, really, Chuck," Ellen said. "I'd feel better if you'd let me drive you to the appointment."

He gave her a charming grin. "I'd rather do it myself," he answered. "I'm looking forward to the ride. And I need some solo time to think all this through."

"Well..." She sounded doubtful.

"Then you won't have to take off work, and your sister will handle Todd."

"She's getting tired of it. If I drove, he could come along."

"She won't have to do it much longer. He'll be in preschool this fall."

"Chuck, I'm worried about you. I'm afraid something might happen on the way."

The confident look he wore began eroding. "I'll be all right. Promise." She shrugged and gave him a half-smile. "Do you have a ten I can carry for gas?" he asked. She did.

"And I'll make you a couple of sandwiches and put in an apple," she said. "You'll need something to eat along the way."

✳

It took Paxton half an hour to get to the interstate before he started to make good time toward Saint Louis. It was one of those utterly clear spring days, hot and just a bit humid. The previous night's rain had scrubbed the air clean, and huge clumps of cumulus were pacing him along the road.

He joined a line of cars and let them set the speed. He loved driving in open country like this, under the great arching sky. It reminded him of some of the motor marches they pulled in Nam. No rice paddies in Missouri, though. He smiled.

About halfway to Saint Louis, a car passed him. The two kids in the back looked at him funny and laughed. He was puzzled for a second, until he checked the mirror and saw that his exhaust had thickened and darkened, and a robust trail of blackish smoke was pouring out behind. He looked at the dash and found the radiator temp was riding high.

He pulled onto the shoulder. He had put an extra quart of oil on the floor of the back seat, expecting to add it for the trip home, but he needed it now—way too soon. He hoped nothing major was going to happen to the car. He didn't have the money to put into it. He stopped at the next rest area, let the radiator cool, found it low, and topped it off with water. The motor pool NCO was going to ream him a new one. Paxton could hear him now: "User maintenance, people, user maintenance. Ninety percent of vehicle problems are caused by a loose nut behind the steering wheel." Paxton smiled now, but he knew he wouldn't be smiling when he got back to base.

When he resumed, he stuck to the right lane and kept it down to 50. A few miles from the city, the smoke came back again, big time. He dropped it to 40, then 35, and finally got inside the city limits. He was cruising below the legal minimum, but no cops bothered him. As he took the Jefferson Avenue off-ramp, the radiator was way over temperature. Cars streamed around and past him, the occupants sometimes glancing at his car.

Then he noticed some kind of gray smoke escaping out the seam between the hood and the fender. He decided that radiator pressure must have ruptured one of the old water hoses. But the gray quickly turned black and oily. In seconds, the paint on the hood began to blister. At the same moment that he realized he had an engine fire, he felt a dull explosion shake the car. He stopped it right in the middle of the street, hastily set the emergency brake and jumped out of the car.

He watched from behind the cover of a parked car on the other side of the street as the fire slowly spread and a crowd gathered. The RPG round had struck the engine dead on, crippling the vehicle and starting the blaze. But they'd made a major error because they didn't seem to have the ambush site covered with small-arms fire. He caught the sound of the fire equipment and just as he turned to see if the trucks were visible, they fired another RPG round. The gas tank exploded and burning fuel began to run down the pavement. He realized they could still have snipers ready to work the area and moved off down the sidewalk.

The fire department had the blaze under control in minutes. As he hung at the edge of the cluster of bystanders, he considered what to do. Isolated as he was, on foot and in strange terrain, he decided that Escape and Evasion was his best course of action. He took an inventory. He had a handful of change, a pocketknife, a handkerchief, and $17 in scrip. No food—and anyway, all he'd brought was the sack lunch Ellen gave him and it burned with the car. He smiled grimly as he thought about survival training and the fine art of goat rustling. But that won't work in these built-up urban areas. So how do you live off the land when it's paved over with tarmac and concrete? He knew he'd be finding out the hard way.

He wondered for a moment whether he'd ever make it safely back to base or see Ellen again. The likelihood of being alone for an extended period weighed heavily and left him sad.

Time to move on, time to find a secure place to logger for the night.

He would miss the boy.

Chapter 7

First Paxton found the Vet center. He got there after his scheduled appointment, but that didn't bother him—he wasn't ready to go in without a careful recon. He hung out close by, so he could watch the comings and goings. He picked a gangway between two buildings, so he'd have cover on his flanks. At the back end of the gangway, he set up a small pile of old cans and bottles so anybody coming around the corner would knock them over and alert him.

A few individuals went in and out during the day, staying an hour or so. Then, right before 5:30, about ten or twelve people straggled in and stayed an hour or so. Same thing at 8:00. Group sessions, he decided.

In between the sessions, he found a supermarket. He loitered till an older woman wheeled her groceries out to the barrier that kept the carts from being taken onto the parking lot and stolen. When she headed out to get her car, Paxton casually walked by her groceries and, without stopping, eased a loaf of bread out of one of the bags. Then he headed back to his gangway and had supper.

When the last group left and the Center had been locked up for the night, he went to the rear parking lot and settled down behind a dumpster. It was better than sleeping on rice paddy dikes, but not much. Before he fell asleep, he decided the Center was probably okay and he would check in soon. Maybe they have coffee and donuts, he thought, and smiled.

Once during the night, the headlights of a car entering at the other end of the parking lot woke him. He was instantly on his feet, and kept the dumpster between him and the vehicle. It was a police car, checking for a light inside or a broken window. There weren't any, and it drove on. That helped Paxton decide not to overnight at the same place twice in a row, if he could help it. And to make sure he had concealment around his sleeping site.

After a couple of days he checked in at the center, but he was distinctly uncomfortable. He didn't like giving up the camouflage of being somebody on the streets, of just blending in. But they had coffee, as he'd hoped, and a large cellophane package of lemon sandwich cookies was still over half full. He grabbed a handful and took a seat, waiting for what they called an intake interview.

He hadn't been there a minute when a man came out of an inner office. "Charles Paxton?" Paxton waved his hand and stood, shoving a last cookie in his mouth. The man held the door open for him, and as he entered the room he took a swallow of coffee to get rid of the cookie faster.

"Have a seat," the man said. "I'm Harold Foster, one of the staff counselors here. Call me Hal." He sat down across from Paxton, scanning the form he'd filled out earlier. "Let's see— Charles John Paxton, single, from Joachim Hill, Missouri— how long a drive is that?"

"Two hours or so," Paxton replied, and took another swallow of coffee to wash down the last of the cookie.

"What do you prefer, by the way—Charlie? Chuck?"

"Chuck."

He continued to look over the form. "Army, eh?" Paxton nodded. "Airborne and infantry." Hal looked at him over his reading glasses. "Lot of action?"

"Yeah."

"So what exactly did you do over there?" He took off the glasses. "What happened?"

"Well," Paxton said, shrugging. He looked away a moment.

What happened? Kessler dead, half his skull strewn across a paddy—that happened. Janowitz missing, probably fertilizing the rice crop—that happened. Captain Bonner, the First Sergeant, hot LZ, gunship down, get that machine gun—

Send your best.

He looked back at Hal. "I was a squad leader," he said.

※

Over a couple of weeks, he learned where the public parks were, and the viaducts that spanned railroad tracks below. He discovered there were a lot of people living the way he did, most of them vets like himself. He figured out how to get away from the drunks without looking unfriendly—they were kind of crazy to talk to, but sometimes they had good info on where to panhandle or sleep. And where the good dumpsters were behind restaurants. Churches ran shelters and served hot meals, and he learned to tap into them, but his security instincts kept him from making it a habit—with all those people, it just wasn't safe.

He particularly liked to overnight at the big botanical garden. Still, he would go there only one night every week or two. Once he got inside the perimeter unseen, he could get far enough away from the streets so he wouldn't be seen. All he had to worry about was getting into vegetation that would prevent the night watchman from spotting him. And he'd make sure to put any food wrappings into a trash can, so there'd be no evidence they were hosting overnight company.

One late summer night, he headed for the garden. He hadn't been there for over two weeks, so he felt safe. As usual, it was a piece of cake to get in. The night was still, with dawn an hour away. The moon, just past full, was starting to set and casting good, deep shadows. All it took was an easy vault over a temporary gate for construction vehicles. He loved the garden when he had it all to himself. Old Henry Sym, one of those wealthy Victorian bachelors, had lavished his fortune on it. Paxton, feeling just a bit cocky, was going to be totally alone there.

During the day, the other garden goers stood patiently in line for tickets like sheep, and carefully followed the walks on their glossy maps. On Sunday mornings, the women came straight from church and, in the face of all logic and comfort, strolled a mile or more of paths in high heels with their gentlemen. He decided no one ever thought about fence jumpers and he felt superior to the coat-and-tie crowd.

He set a wandering route to the grave—first, through the rose garden by the old brick greenhouse with the bust over the door. In the distance, he could see the angels on their poles above a circular pond. He hated them. From here, they looked like they were on the long fall into hell, playing their instruments as they went. He hated them up close, too. Their bodies were too long, too skinny. They were full-grown, but their genitals were hardly developed. Their plumbing reminded him of a picture he'd seen of a barely formed male fetus, almost without a sex. Looking up from behind, there was no round of ripe pear hanging down—only the briefest of twigs, token of a wish to be completed.

Beyond the angels, it was a straight shot to the grave in its fenced circular plot. But the stretch of ground between rose gently, almost 60 meters long, with a broad lawn of close-cropped grass. There was no cover and only spotty concealment, with enough moon to make him twitchy. He cut diagonally right, staying close to a ragged tree line.

He came to a blacktop walk that eventually passed by the grave. He scanned it quickly for danger areas. Farther along was a 20-meter stretch with thick bottlebrush buckeye on either side, restricting lateral movement and inviting enfilading fire down the path. *Thank you, no,* he smiled tautly. He continued across the walkway and 20 paces beyond, then turned left and paralleled it, resuming his approach toward the tomb.

A few meters short of the life-sized mother and child, he stopped. These figures were sure no Jesus and Mary—they were real people. And naked, good. You could see they were real, not like those things stuck up on their poles. The little boy was more male than the angels. And the woman had a good body yet, still well short of 30. Kept her figure, probably her first kid. He smiled a bit—did the sculptor get a few jollies shaping her breasts? He looked at the plaque in the bright moonlight. Probably not, made it at the end of his life, the year before he died. Never know, though. Maybe his dick was the last thing to go. Did he know he was dying, that it was inside him? That would make a dick go limp. Maybe he didn't get off feeling the breasts, maybe it was the stuff he worked in, like when his hands were actually in the clay or whatever. He remembered a sermon Padre gave once about how priests were like carvers and souls were the things they shaped. It was vocation Sunday, and he was playing recruiting sergeant.

He thought he'd like to be a sculptor or an artist, feel something as it actually took shape. Then he realized that soldiers don't make. They call down artillery fire. They burn stuff. Kill. He frowned. Padre, he decided, had been stretching it, saying that priests were artists. God was probably the only real artist. Makes us, sticks us in His garden, like here. Walks through when the sun's almost down and it's getting cool. He pictured an old bearded guy in a long toga sort of thing. Does He notice us when He strolls through? Paxton thought he must have already spent more time here with this woman and her baby than God had ever spent with him. Then why make me or anybody else? Does He get His jollies shaping the clay? Are we just a quick grab and feel? And if we try to push Him away, does He laugh? Maybe He loses it and gets pissed.

"Charles."

He froze, nostrils flaring, hackles rising in the night.

Silence. Then again, louder, "Charles."

Whoever it was had to be very close to the grave. Holding his body absolutely still, Paxton visually quartered the foliage, straining to pick up the slightest movement. He'd empty a magazine into the tree line wherever the bushes moved funny and follow it with a couple of quick grenades. Then, while they fistfucked with that, he'd break contact and haul ass.

But there was no movement, only the pre-dawn stillness and the setting moon. Finally, he began a slow approach to where he thought the voice had come from, keeping trees between himself and the spot. He'd spent ten minutes crossing 30 meters, but now he'd have to hurry. The strengthening twilight was overtaking the moon's illumination, and he was rapidly losing the concealment of darkness. Sweat ran freely down his back and into the cleft of his buttocks, but he was getting close now. He could see the outlines of the gazebo and its windows, sheltering Henry Sym's remains. He put another tree between him and the tomb.

"Charles."

Again he froze, astonished. He was sure the voice had come from inside the gazebo, a Gothic, churchlike little structure just big enough for the raised sarcophagus. The windows and door were glassed, he knew, with a sturdy old lock securing the entranceway, but somebody had to be in there. Slowly, he moved his head till his right eye extended beyond the tree.

"Come here, Charles," the man inside the gazebo said. "It's all right. We're secure."

He made a quick check left and right, then approached the gazebo. Flabbergasted, he looked at the man inside. He and the sculpted tomb figure were identical.

"You're Mister Sym."

"Call me Henry," he said pleasantly.

He noticed that Henry held a rosebud in his right hand, just as the stone Henry did. Only his was real, a fresh and abundant red, newly cut.

"One of the gardeners just brought it," Henry explained, following his gaze. "Every morning, just before the sun comes up, he removes yesterday's wilted rose and inserts today's fresh one into my hand." He motioned with his head toward his own effigy.

The flower fascinated Paxton and he wanted to touch it—softly, gently, feeling the velvet petals give way to delicate pressure. But Henry had indicated his statue on top of the tomb. How could any gardener replace a stone rose? And why would he need to? Then a thought struck him and his eyes narrowed. "He just brought it?"

"Yes."

Paxton stiffened. He knew then that Henry was lying, because he'd have seen the gardener in the moonlight. But the rosebud had to come from somewhere and there were no bushes in sight. Then a new idea hit him and his mouth half opened.

"You're not here." He felt ridiculous, as Henry smiled. "Are you," he added. It was a statement of fact.

"Still, you're talking to me."

"But you're not really here."

"Then, where am I?"

"You know what I mean."

Henry conceded the point with a shrug. "Do you like talking to me?"

He considered a moment. "I think so."

"Then you should probably keep it up."

"Yeah."

"What do you want to talk about?"

Paxton felt dubious, confused. This was crazy, but he hadn't talked to anybody seriously in a long time. The drunks summering in the big park were consumed by wrongs received and needs not filled, and made sense only to themselves. Here at least was someone apparently willing to listen. *Or is he no one?* He felt even more ridiculous and was uncomfortable not saying anything. He looked around.

"Why have they trimmed all the lower branches off that wisteria?"

"It forces the growth upward. Sometimes, they'll even change the shape of a plant into something else. They like to trim rose bushes so they look like little trees."

"But they're not trees."

"Still, the flowers have just as bright a color and smell as sweet."

"I guess."

The pause between them grew into a silence. Paxton glanced at Henry, who seemed content to wait for him to speak. But why try again? Why bother? Right after he got back, the guys down at Herb's acted interested at first, but then they seemed to turn—what? Polite, that was it—polite and bored. He at least thought Al, who'd been in Korea, would understand. But no. Stop trying to remember, Al said, try to forget, and he'd bought a round. *Sure, Al, be glad to forget—where's the off button?* Gradually, Paxton figured out that 'Let me buy you a drink' meant 'Here's some bourbon. Now go talk to somebody else.' It tore at him—to have his past life and present dreams bore people. To reveal at last the sludge that mired him, the muck that pulled him down and sucked at every step, and then be ignored. To be endured by others only with the crutch of another drink. To bore. His eyes welled up and he turned away, angry. God, how he loathed self-pity! *Why bother? Why bother?* To go through this humiliation, forcing himself to talk, and then to bore, to be treated politely: let me buy you a drink.

He could feel Henry watching him quietly. The old man smiled just a bit when Paxton looked at him. Had it come to this? No one who would listen to him, except this phantom? He wondered how crazy he really was. Even in the presence of this man who wasn't there, Paxton felt afraid that he'd find boredom deep in the recesses of those eyes, get an arm's length of politeness for his pains and a glass of beer.

I don't want to do this. I don't.

But he knew he would. Again. His eyes pleaded with Henry's for concern, for connection. His gaze faltered, fell on his helpless fingers. Finally, reluctantly, he shrugged and said, "I was in the war..."

✕

"Does Henry know about the rat?"

Paxton thought a moment. "I never mentioned it," he replied, "but sometimes he seems to know stuff I never told him."

Hal sat thinking that over. As a shrink, he was okay. Ned, another vet, had told him once that the psychologists spent about 12 months at these Vet Center storefronts. Then they went off somewhere with a doublegood bullet for their résumés: I can work cooperatively and effectively in large organizations, the hidden message would say, and I dealt at the cutting edge with the intractable and socially wrenching issue of Our-Veterans-Who-Suffer-From-Combat-Trauma. Paxton smiled slightly, wondering how much longer Hal would be around to keep pestering him about the rat. Sooner or later, they all got stuck on the rat—in Nam before he came home, in the hospital stateside, and now here. Then, before the issue was resolved, they left with varying degrees of regret, depending on their guilt, taking their résumé bullets with them.

127

"If I recall correctly, the rat was in the chalice, right?"

Here we go. "I told you that already." Why were they all fascinated by the chalice?

"Chuck, were you an altar boy when you were a kid?"

"The rat with the wound in his side is not Christ. He's not Satan pissing in the altar wine. He's just a rat. You people, swear to God. He lives off dead soldiers, sucks up their blood, got it? You've all got one-track minds, Jesus."

"If it's just a rat, why didn't it die when you shot it?"

Paxton frowned. He'd dealt with that question himself and still didn't have a good answer. "I don't know," he said after a few moments. "Maybe he's from the same place as Henry."

"What place is that?"

"I don't know!" He surprised himself with the anger, but hoped it masked his fear. If they were both from the same place, he decided a week ago, then Henry was working with the rat. That made things dangerous but simple until he realized that the other place could have good types and bad types, too, and that Henry could very well be okay. That made things dangerous and complicated. He continued to talk with Henry, but watched for the slightest twitch or twinge, any flicker that said he was getting over on Paxton, running some fatal game on him.

"Chuck, when will the rat come out? What will it take to get it to leave?"

Same questions, all of them. "He's not coming out."

"Why not?"

Simple shit. "Because I won't let him."

"Chuck, you can't keep it inside you like that."

"Why the fuck not?"

"Didn't you tell me it tries to get out? Chew its way through?"

"Teeth and claws both, Doc, teeth and claws both." Paxton gave a tight-jawed grin. "But it won't do him any good."

"Chuck, why?"

"Will you stop calling me by my name every third question? Did you guys all take the same bedside manner seminar? And for stupid fucking questions like that. I already told you. It's because he lives on dead soldiers, leeches their blood. If he gets out, he'll go on to the next one and the next and the next."

"But how can you keep going with him in there?"

His eyes dropped. He sat in silence a good 30 seconds, working through the question. "I'll hang in as long as I can, then I'll take him with me."

Evidently, it was something Hal had half expected. "Suicide?" he asked calmly.

These shrinks. "KIA, Doctor Hal."

He ignored the sarcasm. "You'll die in combat?"

Paxton sat in silence.

"Chuck, I can—sorry. But listen now, I can get him out so he won't do any more harm. So he'll never touch another dead soldier."

Paxton looked at him with utter contempt. "You lying son of a bitch." He said it slowly, quietly, with precise articulation, drilling the other's eyes with a palpable loathing.

Hal flushed angrily and started to say something but stopped. He started over and again checked himself. Finally, he said, "But I can."

"You *all* can—if you work with me three times a week for five years. But you've already been here seven months, which means you'll be gone by Christmas at the latest. And if you can do five years of therapy that fast, Doctor Hal, the rat's not Jesus Christ, *you* are." He knew from the fresh surge of color on his face that Hal already knew where he'd be going and when. "Nailed you, didn't I?" Neither of them smiled.

"Look, you don't have to buy the farm to take out the rat."

"Right." Paxton stood and moved leisurely to the door.

"Come back next week."

"I'll think about it."

"I'll keep the hour open for you." And he was gone.

※

When they put the building up decades ago, they carved *Dedicated to Art and Free to All* above the door. "And warm," added Paxton. He pushed through the far set of doors and left the chill December day behind for a while, cutting an immediate right into the section on Mediterranean civilizations. A guard on the opposite side saw him, but Paxton was already into the exhibition area with other visitors, and they didn't like to make a scene when other people were around.

On the way in, he noticed a sign outside the museum shop announcing that there were only six more shopping days until Christmas. It was hard to believe, but this time last year he and his squad were sweating their way across the paddies in Nam, wondering if they'd be back in base camp for a hot meal of turkey and dressing come Christmas, or out in the field munching C rations for their holiday dinner. He went deeper into the exhibition area.

He liked the life-sized statue of the Egyptian cat with a gold earring and wanted to study it a while, but he had to stick fairly close to two mothers convoying five children through the galleries so that the guards would be less likely to challenge him. The kids looked to be between six and ten years old, and he wondered why they weren't in school. The boys were a bit rowdy. When he gave the guard a quick look, she was focused on the kids. One of them dropped a *Guide to the Museum* pamphlet, and Paxton put it in his back pocket to read when he had more time. As he straightened up, he glanced at the guard again and realized for the first time that she was some kind of an Asian ethnic. He scowled. He had learned long ago not to trust Vietnamese women, not even when you were plugged in—*especially* when you were plugged in. If you didn't have your scrip in your hand, old mama-san would be helping herself while you were dropping your load on one of her sweet young things.

When the families turned left down the hall and the guard followed them, he went straight one more room before swinging left himself, into the Chinese landscapes painted on scrolls. He'd have gone in the other direction to shake the guard if he'd had to, but he preferred these peaceful scenes, especially the one of the island with the massive stone mountain thrusting up a hundred feet or so straight out of the water. At first, it seemed all grays when you looked at it, shading at some points down into black. Then, you became aware of the faintest green tinge to the sea, with edgings of whitish foam at the tips of the waves and at the bow of the little boat that a man was rowing toward the island. Then you noticed little touches of the faintest blue in the corners of the sky farthest away from the mountain.

Even for one person, the boat was tiny and looked fragile riding low in the water. You could tell that the man was rowing with all his strength into the mists that masked the shore.

What's on that island for him? He could very well swamp the boat rowing that hard, or smash it into a rock hidden by the drifting mists. He figured the man was hell-bent to get up to a little hut just short of the summit, and he always tried to figure out who or what must be in it. One, maybe two rooms at most. Sometimes, he gave it up. Sometimes, he decided it was a woman, waiting patiently to pour him tea. He thought the elaborate tea ceremony must be some sort of a turn-on for Asian men but could never figure out why.

Then, he realized that the Asian woman, the guard, was in the room with him, and there was no sign of the families. They were alone and his sense of danger was instantly acute. Arms and legs went taut, his pulse flailed, and his saliva suddenly tasted like pennies. He forced himself to move casually, to focus on the landscapes, as he padded slowly out into the hall.

The boys in the next room erupted into shouting and the mothers started yelling at them. The guard hurried past him and into the room. He moved down the hall three or four doors, as quickly as he could without looking like he'd just snatched something. Then he went into a room and he was looking straight at the mask of a Chinese, a priest of some kind—head bald, probably shaved, mouth in the slightest of smiles. He looked straight into the mask's eyes, but they were focused on something beyond and a bit below him. Paxton squatted down until his head was on a level with the mask and followed its gaze to discover what had captured those eyes, but there was nothing to see. The little sign said 'Chinese Mystic, c. 1000 B.C.' What did a Chinese mystic look at, what was out there a thousand years before Christ to hold him like that? He knew if he had come upon the real, breathing man 3,000 years ago, he still wouldn't have seen what it was, though the mystic would still be rapt. Maybe it was the same something in the hut on the mountain, and the man in the boat wanted to see it, too.

The two families came in, bird-dogged by the guard, and he slid into the next room. And he was in the presence of a larger-than-life wooden statue of some Asian, probably a god—sitting relaxed, prime of life, with his fully extended right arm resting across his raised right knee, bent left leg flat on the ground. He was thinking something over—his head leaned slightly to the right, eyes downcast and pensive. Everything was casual, except for the intense look on his face and the formal pose of his right hand, like a ballet dancer's. You could see the folds of his loose skin where the thin garment didn't cover. He didn't get much exercise then, but there was no spare fat. His light clothing lay in carved little ripples, and his long hair hung over his left shoulder. There were double bracelets on each wrist.

This guy doesn't sweat for his food—no work, no worry. Why that intense concentration then? Was he thinking about the same thing as the Chinese mystic? Paxton became perplexed by that something, wanted to see it, too, or at least know what it was. He read the sign: 'Bodhisattva: a highly enlightened being of divine compassion and limitless powers who foregoes the fullness of enlightenment in order to help others.' This guy had gotten right up to the gates of heaven, then, and stopped, so he could give other people a hand. He smiled. What an idea. All Paxton had was Saint Jude, patron of lost causes. Born into the wrong religion, he thought, and his smile widened. He wished this guy had been their chaplain in Nam, then wondered if there were any Buddhist chaplains in the Army. Stuck with old Padre, he thought, and he grinned. He ran his fingers lightly over the carved folds of cloth.

He felt her hand on his arm at the same instant he heard her: "You're not allowed to touch the artworks." Turning, he found her face 18 inches from his own. But when he looked at her, it wasn't the guard. It was the girly whose face was throbbing with hate as he got up off of her. He crumpled the money and threw it between her legs, but he wanted to pound that hatred into terror. Now he continued rounding on the guard, pivoting, seeing only the whore's hating face. He uncoiled the heel of his left hand with enormous force directly into her mouth. A spurt of blood shot outward and down in a graceful little arc, spattering on his thigh. She was unconscious before the blow had slammed her against the wall. She slid to the floor with blood and saliva spilling from her mouth and over her lower lip. He'd probably broken her jaw.

He took three seconds to assess. She had no weapon, no communications. He checked the ceiling. There were movement sensors, but no video cams. He smiled grimly—should have been an art thief. The kids were getting louder and would be in the room in another second. He went through the other door and paused. To his right was an entrance onto an open-air sculpture court. Across the court, there was another door going into the restaurant. Behind him, one of the little girls screamed for her mother. Ignoring the sculpture garden for a moment he moved straight ahead a dozen paces to an exit marked 'emergency only—alarm will sound.' As soon as he pushed it open, a klaxon kicked on and he retraced his steps. That should keep them busy, he thought, and headed toward the door to the sculpture court.

As he passed the doorway to the Bodhisattva's room, one of the mothers screamed, "There, that's him!" and two male guards grabbed him, one behind, keeping his arms pinned, the other trying to pull his legs out from under him. The guy around his legs he kicked in the face, sending him sprawling, then he twisted half left and brought his elbow up hard, an uppercut on the point of the jaw that made the guy behind him let go fast. He turned back to the first man, who was on his feet again and coming at him, and caught him with a chop to the throat that would keep him tame for a while. Then the guy behind him again—Paxton uncoiled his left leg in full extension, his combat boot catching the guard square in the stomach. Then he hammered him once on the temple with the base of his fist and he went down. He had tried to pull his punches. These guys were basically noncombatants. But he had to get the hell out of there.

He walked on quickly and out into the sculpture court, leaving the hysterical women and five screaming kids standing over the guards. The klaxon droned on.

He immediately pushed through the farther door into the restaurant and brushed past a woman with an armful of menus.

"Sir. Sir!"

He ignored her, pausing just long enough to rip out the wiring of her phone, then he strode straight into the kitchen. Food prep, cleanup, door to the outside. Just like a mess hall. He passed a guy wearing a chef's hat, mouth gaping at him, and continued out onto the loading dock. One of the restaurant helpers was throwing some last bags of garbage into the back of a huge trash truck making a metallic diesel din. The driver was just getting into the cab when Paxton thrust past the helper and jumped off the dock. As the truck started to pull away he sprang onto the right rear platform where any extra crew could ride.

They picked up speed, the wind lashing his face with his own tangled hair. He closed his eyes and was sitting in the door of a slick at 2,000 feet, heading back to base after a nasty firefight. When he opened his eyes, he was looking at the still wet bloodstains on his pants, and he knew the leeches were back, under the OD cloth of his uniform. Or was the blood not his own, but Kessler's? Maybe both. He looked far down at the lovely, deceptive symmetry of the rice paddies. He stared at the hopeful green below, lying with its promise of plenty and freedom from a belly torn by pain, while he and Kessler mingled their blood in the damp smear on his filthy pants. And the pull to stand up and step off the runner of the bird came strong over him. Thrust the wind aside, shatter the air with the force of his falling, overmaster it for a few endless moments—like the last few seconds of sex that seem like they'll never end, but do. They do end. Pieces of time conclude and when you open your eyes, you're inches from a Vietnamese whore's face and she's got your sap and your money both, and tomorrow her soldiers will be doing their best again to kill you, to splash your brains and your blood on the GI behind you, and he won't ever be free of it, won't ever be able to wash it away.

The truck geared down noisily, climbing a hill, and he looked around. The service road ran through a wooded, thickly grown section of the park not far from his place. He waited till the truck, moving slowly, had just crested the hill and started down the back side, and jumped.

135

He stood in the road on the reverse slope of the hill for a second, watching the truck speed away. He had to get to the dry streambed in front of him at the bottom of the hill. Twenty meters up the stream was his place. He had it well concealed and he'd probably be okay there unless they brought in tracker dogs. Right now, he had to decide whether to trot straight down the road—it would take him about 45 seconds—or move off into the thick undergrowth and work down through the terrain. Doing it right would take at least ten minutes, maybe more, and cops would be buzzing around here any second. He set off along the road at an easy jog and a minute later, he was working his way up the dry bed, moving carefully so as not to turn over any rocks. To anyone who could read signs, those white rock underbellies would shout, "This way!"

At the mouth of the cave, he stooped, located the tripwire and stepped carefully over it. He learned how to set up the rig from Dinh, an NVA soldier who had taken the *chieu hoi* option and become a Kit Carson scout, a turncoat who tracked his own people, helped interrogate prisoners and made himself generally useful. Dinh particularly liked running the questioning when two NVAs were taken. After the pair had been secured, he would come into the tent alone, saying nothing. Without a word, he would slowly take out his .45 and calmly shoot the first prisoner, always at the base of the throat, right in the V of the bone. It took the man almost a minute to die, and he made the noisy sucking and gurgling sounds that put the second prisoner in a mood to tell Dinh whatever he wanted to know.

The first time Paxton realized what was going on, he'd brought in the prisoners himself directly from the field and was sticking around to stretch his break from operations a bit. At the sound of the shot, he rushed into the tent, rifle ready. The man lay on the ground, bleeding profusely from the wound, with blood bubbling raspily out of his mouth. The other prisoner wore a mask of stark terror and made little squeaks of fear with his exhalations. Smiling ever so faintly, Dinh held the pistol patiently in his right hand, cradling its muzzle in the crotch of his left thumb and forefinger. He waited for the prisoner to tear his eyes away from his dying friend and read his fate in Dinh's face. Paxton couldn't fathom a man who would do that to his own people and was awed by his cold-bloodedness when he worked. A captain had come in a few minutes later and said something about another one trying to escape. Dinh then told him the company, battalion and regiment that the two were from, who commanded each echelon, when they had left North Vietnam, how far and how quickly they had come, the effectiveness of American interdicting fires en route, and how bad the dysentery was.

On a patrol one evening just before dusk, Dinh had shown him how to emplace the tripwire rig. In less than 20 minutes, using the whipping effect of a young tree, he'd cocked and set the device. The patrol then set up an ambush along the most likely avenue of enemy withdrawal from the booby trap. That night, they heard the *twang-thump* of the rig and the screams of a wounded soldier that quickly subsided. Sixty seconds later, Dinh let the point man of the enemy patrol pass him, then initiated the ambush by stitching him up the back with half a magazine of M16 on full automatic. There were another seven KIAs in the main killing zone, including the guy who had been caught in the rig. In addition to two spike wounds, he'd been hit by three M60 machine gun rounds. Paxton asked Dinh later why they had carried the dead man with them after they took him off the rig. Dinh only shrugged, as if he didn't understand it himself. He said, "They do that sometimes." Once in the cave behind the rig, Paxton felt safe.

Three minutes later, he heard someone stumble and send a rock clattering back downhill toward the road, accompanied by a fervent "shit." He moved slowly until he could see through the bushes covering the low mouth of the cave. A cop down in the streambed was working his way up toward Paxton's place. The officer must have seen him leave the road and followed him into the undergrowth.

Paxton considered his options. He could go out the back way, but any sound at all would put the cop right on his heels. His one hope was that the other would miss the thickly overgrown opening. Then he sucked in his breath, his heart pounding. The museum pamphlet lay on the ground right in front of the cave. He reached back and touched his empty pocket, cursing his carelessness, but it was too late.

The officer probably thought Paxton was a wino or maybe a queer out for a quick one in the bushes, but he was going to check it out. The cop stopped. If he called for his canine patrol, Paxton would have to go out the back anyway and take whatever came. Then Paxton saw his eyes fasten on the pamphlet. As he eased sideways from the cave entrance, he watched the cop's foot poke at it. When the officer realized there was a small cave entrance behind the bushes, he pushed the undergrowth aside with his hand. He couldn't know how far back it went because his eyes weren't used to the inner darkness. The cop drew his weapon.

Paxton watched him start to bend low to go through the entryway and then hesitate. *Wait for your backup.* But he pushed through and straightened up, pausing a few seconds for his eyes to get used to the dark. Paxton was in deep shadow to his right and slightly behind him. He watched as the cop made out the shopping cart with clothes and some groceries in it, and against the far wall the sleeping bag and a couple of empty food cans. The officer's face visibly changed in the dim light, as he realized that somebody called this home. He went one more step into the cave.

At the *twang-thump,* Paxton was instantly at his side, one hand over his mouth to muffle the screams, the other taking the weapon out of his hand so it wouldn't go off and alert someone. He had improved the rig by replacing the sapling with some coiled metal springs he scavenged. The length of 2x4 had hit with enormous force, and the 20-penny spikes embedded in the wood had struck simultaneously in the chest, belly and groin. The wounding had been savage. Within seconds, the man was hanging limp.

He threw the gun into a far corner of the cave. Carrying it would just be a red flag. There was no use wiping it clean, his fingerprints were on everything. Taking hold of the body, he lifted it off the spikes and lowered it gently to the earth. His right hand came away dripping, and he wiped it grimly on his pants. He looked down at his hand, rubbing blood into blood, and with a flash of realization he knew the officer was a part of him and Kessler now. Could never be separated from them.

Paxton studied his face. He was young, a long way from 30. The nametag on his pocket flap read 'M.J. Schneiderman.' M.J.—a good handle. There was no wedding ring, but Paxton wondered anyway if he was married—or had children, or wanted to. He closed the eyes and let his hand rest on M.J.'s cheek. Pain and surprise had frozen on the face. The three of them might have been in the same squad—Paxton, Kessler and M.J. He wanted more than anything for this not to have happened, and his eyes welled. *Friendly fire,* he thought, pushing a strand of hair back from the dead man's forehead. *I'm killing my own people.* He sensed the rat beginning to stir inside, amused. The blood would never stop. His heart sank. His hands would always be in blood.

Quiet for weeks, the rat went taut and vicious, goaded by the death smell. *Don't worry,* Paxton promised M.J., *I won't let him out. He won't get you.* At that the raw, frantic slashing inside him doubled and redoubled, the rat mad to be at this fresh new blood. Paxton crossed the dead man's hands on his chest in the face of stupefying pain, then sat clutching his belly, knowing with an unshakable certainty that he would never live his life apart from violent death. The rat would see to that, draw him irresistibly to bloody dying, pull him to it again and again, till Paxton was too weak to hold him inside any more and he'd escape. Paxton looked at the gun in the corner. Maybe now. Maybe right now. "Through the mouth is best." Ned had told him that. But no. The rat would escape through his own wound and have them both.

He heard voices down at the road. He reached through the opening and pulled in the museum pamphlet, then grabbed a few things from his stash. He gazed tight-lipped a second at M.J., then headed for the rear of the cave. Following a bend left, he was soon outside. He kept going up the culvert, went under cover again into a tunnel of fallen trees and packed earth. At its end, he headed straight west for the nearest boundary of the park, making a point of being seen and yelled at on the golf course. When he was two streets beyond the park, he turned north and moved as quickly and inconspicuously as he could for a couple of streets. He then turned east, paralleling the park at a distance. With any luck, they wouldn't find the dead officer for a good while, and the false trail at the golf course would buy him some more time.

That evening, just at dark as the snow was beginning, he came to ground in the botanical garden by Henry's tomb.

Chapter 8

"**W**hat could I do?"

It was well past midnight. Paxton sat on the ground distraught, as he had for many hours. He leaned against the back section of the gazebo, while his mind searched the day's events, seeking vainly for a different outcome. The right half of his body, away from the gazebo's overhanging roof, was accumulating a covering of wet snow that fell steadily through the moonless night. His left was untouched. Henry, patient but intent, sat inside the gazebo, his own left side against the wall they shared.

As he told Henry about M.J., he became aware of a deep aching inside. It wasn't the rat's pain this time. He knew remorse when it was on him, and right now it was an enormous weight. When he admitted that the young officer was a member of his own squad, tears came, and they still clung tenuously to his cheek, growing cold against his skin. Yet, strangely, he was at a vast remove from the remorse and its tears—like observing some other person from a great distance, glancing out a train window and seeing a cemetery, catching an instant of grief on the face of some stranger standing at the lip of the pit. Mourner and mourned, tears and casket all sharply clear for a moment, but devoid of significance or connection to the observer.

"*You* killed him?" Henry asked incredulously.

Paxton, in agony at Henry's candid disbelief, nodded his admission.

The old man sat in stunned silence for long moments. Then, in a transparent attempt to ease Paxton's remorse, he said halfheartedly, "Well, don't be too hard on yourself. You didn't have many choices."

For a long while, Paxton said nothing, the grief keening inside him. Although the feeling was rooted in M.J., he couldn't visualize his face. In his mind's eye, he saw only a lone pair of combat boots standing by an M16, muzzle to the ground, stuck fast in the earth by its bayonet and topped by M.J.'s helmet. This disembodied grief, without any dilution, began to yield its place, pushed from the center of his awareness toward its darker edges by another feeling. He also knew shame when he saw it and he was looking at it now, vivid and personal, sharply and cleanly connected.

Send your best squad leader.

No one could hold Paxton in more contempt for killing a member of his own squad than he did himself, or be more angry with him. Disgraceful, despicable. Then the remorse at the death, as strong as ever, was joined by contempt. Paxton felt himself being whipsawed by them—remorse and contempt, remorse and contempt—like two roustabouts he'd seen once in a movie, driving a tent stake tandem into the ground, their sledges pounding in turn, pounding, never missing a beat, relentless. And hovering behind it all was the rat, as patient as Henry, maybe more, radiating a coldness outward from its very center, chilling Paxton's whole body from the inside out. Everything inside was slowing down, except the remorse and contempt, remorse and contempt. Everything was grinding slower and slower, the pace of a glacier, a lump of ice. Then his head snapped back in realization.

He lurched to his feet in panic, swayed perilously close to falling, grabbed onto the iron grillwork that protected the gazebo and steadied himself. "Henry," he whispered urgently, "I almost fell asleep. I was freezing to death and I almost fell asleep." *In this kind of war the enemy's everywhere, everything wants to kill you.*

He looked at Henry. He hadn't moved. "Henry!" There was no answer. He tried not to panic. "Wake up. Walk around. Don't give in to it. Don't let it get you!" Still, there was no response, no movement. His hands slid down the grillwork as he sank to his knees. "Henry," he rasped desperately into his ear, "wake up." The older man was patient but intent, his staring eyes focused on the place where Paxton's face had just been. He looked at this Henry who was no longer Henry, nothing remaining but the outer shell, nothing of substance inside now at all. This was no death by freezing. Henry had been called back. Paxton's eyes filled with tears and his lips began to tremble. "Please, Henry," he whispered. "Don't leave me." But he was gone, never to return. Paxton slumped back onto his heels, lowering his head against the bars of the iron grillwork he clung to, and sobbed quietly in the face of this abandonment.

He was utterly alone now. There was no one else, not a single connection remained. Why hadn't he just given himself to the cold and fallen asleep? He tried to think through Henry's departure and decided he'd been recalled to punish Paxton for killing M.J. It was a harsh punishment, excruciating, but when he remembered the hurt and surprise on M.J.'s dead face and saw again his own hand push the hair back from his forehead, there was nothing he could say. *No excuse, Sir.*

Using the grillwork, he pulled himself to his feet and hung on to it to hold himself steady. The night landscape was lurid, the snow gleaming unnaturally in the moonless night. The perverse white covered everything, smothering the earth and all its contents. It seemed impossible to him that anything could ever grow again. He was sure he'd never see another spring.

He stumbled from the gazebo enclosure, following the path wherever it took him. He knew his footprints in the snow were putting him at risk, but he didn't care. *There's all kinds of ways to go to sleep.*

He came to the limb of a tree that was normally overhead, but which now hung almost at eye level from the weight of the wet snow. He paused and stared. Fragments of childhood drifted swiftly through his mind: hearing other kids shouting on the playground before he turned the corner and could see them; a frigid wind flicking his ears as his sled careened hellbent for the bottom of the hill. All those childhood events and sensations—going for it full bore and laughing, taking the *Dare you!* challenge with exhilaration and adrenaline and laughter—and all of it bound together with little-boy fear, covered over with little-boy bravado. They all hovered there beyond the snow-bent branch, just out of his reach. He could see them and hear them and feel the sharp coldness dulling the boy's face to happy numbness, but he couldn't recognize them as his own any more. It seemed incredible to him that he was the boy on the sled, impossible. The man that he now was pondered the boy in front of him with a detached fascination. He considered who he'd become and realized that his manhood's *now* had no emotional linkage to his childhood's *then*; that he'd become someone who, in literal truth, had never been a child. His life hovered there, a series of discrete and separate moments, all of which moved somehow toward his present—yet none of which seemed connected to any of the others and existed only as variations on the struggle to survive. Back then, survival meant taking the dare, fitting in. In the present, it sometimes meant begging, sometimes stealing, and always, sooner or later he knew now, it meant killing. Such a man could never have been a child; could never have played in the snow. He reached up and touched the branch. His memories vanished as a three-foot section of damp snow fell at his feet, like so much clabbery white batter spilled on the kitchen floor. He stared at the soppy pile a long moment, then scattered it into wet chunks with a vicious kick.

He started for the mother and child, but stopped when he realized they'd be sheathed with the stifling snow. He stood there a full minute then, watching the white stuff accumulate on him. If he stayed still long enough, it would sheathe him, too. He turned and went back the way he'd come, setting his feet in the tracks he'd made walking in the other direction. He passed the entrance into the gazebo enclosure and continued on until he was looking at a stand of bamboo 12 feet high, green in all that white. He wanted to feel hope, searched himself desperately for it, but all he could sense was the unnaturalness of those stalks pushing up green through the snow; of pliant life caught in that once and for all, sleep and forget, white covering. He walked on more slowly till he reached the bridge of the carp.

He leaned his elbows on the railing, compressing the snow into thin, dense pats. As far as he could tell, the whole lake was frozen over except for the circle of open water that extended out from here for 15 or 20 feet. It was here that the regular garden goers came to feed the carp. Parents lined up in front of the dispenser at the end of the bridge, waiting to drop in a coin for a handful of fish food to give to their kids. They'd throw the pellets into the water one or two at a time, till 15 or 20 huge carp clustered in front of the bridge in a roiling mob, trying to suck in the pellets. Just about then, one of the boys would scatter a whole handful at once across the seething bodies and pandemonium would take over. The carp would maneuver ponderously around, every mouth a great gaping O, bumping into each other, pushing each other aside, swimming up and over each other, trying to inhale the floating pellets before the flick-flick of a bluegill's mouth and tail beat them to it. It was the incessant turbulence of the water during the day that probably kept this piece of the lake from freezing over.

He scrounged up half-a-dozen pellets from around the base of the machine and began throwing them slowly, one by one, into the lake. Nothing happened. They hung suspended on the water's face, between the two worlds, making delicate little rings on the water. Although the carp kept the surface agitated in daylight, they apparently wouldn't respond at night. *Got a good union. Do fish hibernate? Maybe they've finally started their winter's sleep. Rehearsing for death,* he decided. *Death's a long hibernation.* The rat began stirring restlessly. *What's the spring?* He was almost out of pellets. He threw another into the water and thought about the Bible story of the manna in the desert: how God had fed the chosen people by making bread come down like snow. Or ashes. He let his last pellet drop into the lake. Deep in the water, the tapering shape of a smudgy white carp began to loom. It stopped half a foot from the pellet, but wouldn't feed. Paxton gazed at the dim mass hovering in the depths and wondered if the carp thought he was God delivering a ration of manna. That brought a sad smile and a slow shake of the head. If Paxton was as lousy on behalf of the fish as God was on his, then he and the carp were in serious trouble. But maybe God had to endure this kind of neglect, too. What's God's manna? And who, he wondered, is God's God?

He left the fish submerged in its frigid indecision and walked on, feeling as listless and uninspired as the carp. He wished that worried him, but it didn't; realized he didn't care that it didn't. The rat stirred again, more sharply. In another minute, he'd be wide awake again, trying to escape. Paxton had been out in the weather for at least 15 hours and eaten only a candy bar that he'd snatched up on his way out of the cave. He wasn't sure he was strong enough to keep him inside now, to hold him at bay. As he picked up the pace, the rat began his clawing—not a full-fledged drive to get out, just letting Paxton know he was active. Paxton gritted his teeth at the beginnings of the pain. The rat was playing with him.

Soon, his brisker pace had carried him around to the other end of the lake and its source. He was right. The entire rest of the lake was frozen. But here the stream that fed it still flowed down freely from the waterfall. Twice as tall as a man, the rock face of the falls was draped now with a mass of ice, but the water continued to slide between it and the rock into a kind of collecting pool. From there, it ran down a fair little incline for a last 30 or 40 feet before it fed the lake. Three stepping-stones led across the rivulet.

As he became fascinated by the stream, the rat fell still. The grim recollection of the creek below the Tan Son Nhut mortuary pushed up into his consciousness, and he suddenly became afraid of this little stream, though no less fascinated. And the pull came strong in him to take the path and cross the stream. As it grew, his fear intensified into a kind of controlled terror. He started down the path, his heart beating rapidly.

At the edge of the water, he halted abruptly, realizing that the possibility of being splashed petrified him. The near and far stepping-stones were dry, but the one in the middle was wet, with some ice crystals on it, slippery. What if he fell into the water? He watched it a moment. Every so often, a few drops would splash up and over the stone. It was hardly enough to cover the bottom of a glass, but he was mesmerized by it and starkly afraid.

He forced himself to step onto the near stone, his churning pulse audible inside his head. He waited, watching the middle stone carefully. Just after a bit of water splashed over it, he made his move—left foot on the middle stone, right on the far stone and up onto the shore. He turned, a smile of victory and relief on his face, to gloat and preen before the stream. Grinning triumphantly, arms akimbo, he surveyed the stream from its mouth at the lake up to the top of the hill. As his eyes reached the hill's rim, the water spilling over it darkened and turned an unmistakable crimson. At the sight of it, he exhaled audibly. Then, he said, very quietly, "Oh God," as he caught sight of the rat. It was next to the stream just to one side of a bush near the top of the hill. Its sharp red eyes were on him, mocking him.

He made himself look at the boundary between the water and the blood, as it flowed rapidly down the hill to the mouth of the lake. He wanted to flee this horror, even as he was drawn back to the very edge of the stream to search its depths. He fervently hoped the things he looked for in the wine-dark flow wouldn't be there, but they were. A blind unseeing eye swirled in the current like a marble, a severed finger bumped gently into stones, genitals were wedged between a section of submerged tree branch and the bank, a cleanly lopped hand clung by the crook of its ring finger to a sunken twig, an ear scudded saucerlike on the stream until, filling with tinted water, it sank down to the pebbled bottom. The rat at the top of the hill now sucked at the red drink of the stream, in at the muzzle, out at the jagged wound Paxton had given him. He was brazenly fouling the blood of dead soldiers, flaunting his freedom from Paxton and his contempt for the dead.

Paxton stood there, stunned by the horrific landscape he hoped he'd never see again. The one constant that had kept him going was that as long as he endured the pain, the rat was his captive. He would pay a price, as indeed he had, but the rat was his. It couldn't escape to violate dead soldiers. Now there it sat, taunting Paxton, torturing him with its obvious freedom. He couldn't grasp why or how it had all come about.

All he was aware of was the sudden and pervasive hopelessness flooding in on him now. How many times he'd stood on the brink of despair from the weight of the evil burden inside, but had endured it because he believed it would prevent the very thing that was happening right now, the desecration of soldiers' blood by this rat, this sewer thing. And all for nothing—for nothing. The clawing lacerated his belly again, but the rat was up on the hill, not inside at all. He couldn't understand it. The ease with which the rat had swept away his one remaining certainty was incomprehensible to him.

His belly contracted in pain. He wanted to vomit but couldn't. He stumbled a few steps to a kind of stone column with a Japanese spirit house on top of it that loomed just above his head. He grabbed hold of the column and hung on, and found himself looking straight at the relief of a stag carved on the pillar, with its head, topped by regal antlers, turned to look back over its flanks, searching for something behind it. Paxton knew what he was looking for—the hunter. This was the very moment when the stag realizes the hunter will win. His numbed fingers lost their grip on the frigid stone and he fell heavily to the ground, his face in the snow.

Got to get out of here. The rat still squatted by the stream, watching him, grinning. *Got to get up.* As he pushed himself up onto his elbows, a wad of snow fell from his collar onto the back of his neck and the shock of this new kind of pain clarified his mind for a second. *More snow.* He scooped up a handful and dropped it down his back. His skin shivered and contracted involuntarily, like a horse attacked by flies. He felt his mind clearing. *Got to get away from here.* As he opened his coat, he looked back at the rat sucking greedily at the stream. *In through the muzzle, out at the wound. Got to move.* He rubbed his chest with a handful of snow, then held it against his left nipple, which stiffened in pain. *Good.* He scooped up more snow and struggled to his feet. *Got to get away from here.*

He scrambled up the hill toward the walk, stumbled to his knees but kept going, regained his footing and reached the path, staggered to a tree and hung on. His breath came shallow and rapid, somewhere between gasps and sobs. His gorge began contracting spasmodically, and he knew that at last he was going to vomit. His retchings were dry at first, then the contractions thrust a small amount of viscous liquid up and out. It lay on the surface of the snow, a few wisps of vapor rising off of it. The straggle of red in grayish green confirmed the taste of blood and bile. He had the conviction that his juices were devouring his own body, painfully dissolving him from the inside out. It was the only thing he could think of that would explain the continuing pain in the absence of the rat. Paxton could flee the stream, but he knew he could never leave that behind.

⋇

"We sent the prints to Washington. They identified him as Charles John Paxton, Vietnam vet. Silver Star, that's a pretty big one. Two Bronze Stars, two Purple Hearts. Lots of combat. Which makes people funny sometimes. And that fits with how he killed my officer. The rig's called a death fall, gets a lot of play in guerrilla wars. When we called, your secretary said you've got a patient by that name. Is he the guy we want?"

Hal studied the man across from him, a detective captain who, to look at, could pass for a stockbroker. But the intense, tightly held anger radiated in waves, and the connection implicit in 'killed my officer' resonated with the same buddy loyalty that drove so many veterans into his office.

"There's no way for me to know that."

"But is he capable of it?"

How far could he go without violating his obligation of confidentiality to Paxton? In the context of his legal obligations, he had a duty to warn authorities if someone were in imminent

150

danger from Paxton. To his knowledge, no one was, but he'd have held to that before the officer was killed, too. "I doubt it."

"Was that a definite no, or a squishy 'could be'?"

"This may come as a shock, but I can't see the future. And I don't have personal knowledge of events I haven't witnessed."

The cop held Hal's eyes for a moment, measuring him. "Where does he hang out?"

Hal realized that the detective already knew what his confidentiality limits were, as well as his legal obligations, and he wasn't going to be constrained by either of them. Hal resented being caught between the anvil and hammer of professional ethics and the law—especially being put in this position so close to his departure. The movers were coming next Monday to pack. "Well, the park, of course...."

"Tell me something I don't know." The tone was sharp, distinctly nasty.

"I don't think you'll find him in any of the shelters. He doesn't like to travel with a lot of other people and he doesn't like to stay more than one or two nights in the same location. It's a tactical attitude he developed in Nam."

"What locations does he frequent during the day?"

"Well, his standing appointment here is on Thursday afternoons at 1:00."

"And he didn't show last week. When are you going to tell me something I haven't heard from your secretary?"

"I'm sure you realize I'm dealing with issues of patient confidentiality in the absence of imminent danger, and what kind of trust he'll have in me if I'm the one who..."

"Doctor." He ran his hand down the face of his tie to smooth away its nonexistent wrinkles. "Let me make one thing clear to you." If he were the stockbroker he so much resembled, he'd be getting ready to tell Hal about a major disaster in his portfolio. "I really don't give a shit about your sacred obligation to this guy. His killing skills have been honed razor sharp in combat. He's off the deep end, and I'm not going to risk one more cop unnecessarily to take this guy, not one. And you—if you withhold information that might reduce our risk, then you're making my officers vulnerable, Doctor, and I won't take that lightly. Not lightly at all."

Hal sensed an ultimatum coming. His pulse picked up noticeably. He could feel the color rising in his face and hoped the detective didn't see it. "Look, before you do something stupid like threaten me, don't you think we should..."

"Doctor," he cut in again. His right hand rose like a traffic cop's. Why had Hal said stupid? Why hadn't he said *anything* but stupid?

"The man means nothing to you," the detective said coldly. "This time next month, you hope to be in Boston getting ready to open a private practice. He'll be passed around among the other staff here until someone inadvertently gets stuck with him."

"Did you say I *hope* to be in Boston?"

"Sharp ears. Yes, I did say that, didn't I?"

"There's something that could delay me?"

"Yes." He stopped, forcing Hal to ask him the obvious.

"Well?"

Hal's flushed face was evidently very satisfying to the detective. "You're a material witness, Doctor. You're mine for a long enough period that you'll be paying rent in both places with no job, and your hopeful little project in Boston will lose significant momentum as each day passes."

"I'll take you to court."

"Do that, when it reopens after the Christmas break. And I'll still be able to hold you for a while because you *are* material to this case. You and I both know how loosely patient confidentiality can be construed in these situations. And I don't have to keep you here forever to hurt you. Five or six weeks will do. Anything after that is gravy."

Hal had the repetition of an insight he got from time to time—that his crazies were solid human beings by and large, with a few heavy-gauge problems, and that the sane ones often needed long and intensive help that might well, in the end, prove fruitless.

"Well?"

"He likes the botanical garden. He goes in over the fence after they close and has the place to himself."

"It's a big garden."

"He hangs out around the grave."

"What, Henry Sym's tomb?"

"Yes."

"Why in the world do that?"

"He, uh—he likes to talk things over with Henry."

The detective looked at Hal in frank disbelief. "With *Sym?*"

"Yes."

This was too much even for the stockbroker's facade. "But he's been dead a hundred years!"

"Yes."

"Jesus Christ, Doctor. Didn't it occur to you that a man who talks things over with dead people might need a little special attention? That he should be in some facility and not on the streets? That he might even be dangerous?"

"How did you vote last election?"

"What?"

"Law and order, right? The let's-get-tough-on-crime bunch?"

"Make your point."

"Glad to. Right after they got in, they decided it was too expensive to keep open the kind of facility this guy needs. The day I got him to agree to commit himself, the wait for any kind of bed was three weeks. And by the time the space came open, he'd changed his mind. It was after that when your officer was killed, and now you're going to hunt him down and blow him away. All he has to do is scratch an ear funny and you'll say you thought he was going for a gun."

"Please. Spare me your knee-jerk, liberal-ass crap. He cost that woman guard several teeth, another one's got a concussion, and the third has a ruptured larynx and may never talk again. And he hit all these people, Doctor, maybe half-a-dozen times *total*. The woman he hit only once. He could have killed all of them with nothing but his hands, and I don't really know why he didn't. Then, he turned the park into a combat zone. My officer left traffic control at a school crossing and walked into a death fall. He's got a 26-year-old widow and two boys who aren't even in kindergarten yet. And you think I'm going to have to cook up a story to take him out? He's still deep in some combat zone, and you know it. I'll have to work my ass off *not* to kill him."

"He's dead, isn't he? You're going to do it."

"We'll take him alive if we can, but I'm not losing anybody else to a combat crazy. If his *eyebrow* twitches funny, he's dead." He stood. "Like my cop." He slipped into his overcoat. "You want to tell me anything else, Doctor Boston-Bound?"

Hal paused a second. He hated this man—his everything's right or everything's wrong bent of mind, the roughshod way he achieved his goals. And the worst part of it was, he was right about Paxton. They had turned the Ratman into a killer and set him loose in Vietnam, and now he can't find his way back.

"We run support groups for the vets here, two evenings a week. He's not a regular, but he shows up every so often."

"When's the next one?"

"Tonight."

CHAPTER 9

With the first hint of light, the snow let up and dawn came to a sky unexpectedly cloudless. The air was colder but drier, even crisp. He sat on a bench a few feet from the gazebo. In Paxton's absence, the hollow shell of Henry had apparently shivered into pieces, the fragments turning, in the process, into rose petals of intense red. At least that's what he found when he returned from the lake: a tight scatter of petals on the floor next to the tomb, just visible in the gloom. Paxton was grateful to Henry for this gift. The old man had to go back—orders are orders—but he was under no obligation to leave such an affectionate message of farewell. Paxton sent him a mental thanks. Nevertheless, Henry was gone, and that still hurt. He missed him deeply.

Understandable, but now he had to formulate a plan. Difficult to think—read enemy intentions, analyze one's own capabilities, overlay both on the variables of weather and terrain. One thing for sure—he strongly sensed their intent to pin him against the river, the eastern boundary of the city. Yesterday, they had deprived him of the park, pushing him east. He'd loggered here in the garden last night against his better judgment. His sensing was that the garden was no longer secure and might well be the objective for a search-and-clear operation today. He'd stopped here partly because he needed to rest, but mostly because he wanted to talk things over with Henry. Now, this last motivation no longer applied. His only option was east toward the river. His tactical area of operations was continuing to shrink. He could probably force a crossing, but he knew they also held the opposite bank in strength. And although he had a direction, he knew he didn't really have a plan. He had tactics but no strategy.

And with the rat now gone, what was the source of this continuing pain? What else was inside him? He watched a robin scratch through the snow, down to a layer of last fall's leaves, and send them flying with quick snaps of its head. It wolfed down the odd holly berries it came across, and then it snatched up a still, white grub, hardly moving from the chill, and swallowed it whole. He imagined the robin getting some kind of primitive pleasure from the blind stirrings of the thing in its belly. But could the grub fight back, trapped inside? Strip off the robin's innards in small precise rows, like a caterpillar on a leaf? Could the eaten devour the eater, cut away stomach and spleen? Consume the heart, or burrow so deep inside that, despite its will to go on, it had no option but to cease?

He looked for the robin, but it was gone, its place taken by a squirrel rooting for acorns. But there was something wrong with it. It was scrawny and emaciated, and would pause in place and rest for long moments at a time. Once, it actually heeled over, rolling slowly onto its side in the snow. Maybe it was old or sick, or it was a bad year for food and it was starving. The squirrel righted itself and slowly made its way over to a tall oak and began to climb. It didn't seem in pain, just very tired. At about 30 feet, it achieved a major branch and began crawling out onto it. The branch reached to within a few feet of its neighbor, another oak. Had the squirrel gone up the wrong tree? Paxton gave the neighbor a visual check. At about 20 feet, he spotted an opening in the trunk that he was sure the squirrel wanted to get to. He looked back just as the squirrel, at a narrowing part of the branch, slid slowly sideways again, hanging by all fours to the underside, like a recruit on the rope crawl deciding whether to just let go and fall into the lake. But the squirrel didn't have a lake. It hung there a brief while, then finally righted itself. It made several false starts along the branch, as if trying to gather momentum for a jump. Finally, it sprang off and out, landed on a branch of the neighboring tree, hung on and stabilized itself, and crawled slowly inside the trunk to its nest.

Why didn't it just go straight up its nesting tree? Maybe security, to throw off any predators about where its den was. Regardless, it was in pretty bad shape. What if it died inside the tree? Would the other squirrels put it out? He remembered, without the faintest trace of amusement, the joke you could tell about Rangers or Marines or rugby players, and wondered if squirrels ate their dead. Reluctantly, he decided they probably did.

Just then, out of the corner of his eye, he glimpsed a blur of movement at the nesting tree and caught sight of the squirrel as it hit the earth. When he got to it, it was lying on its side in the snow, conscious, and apparently in no pain. But it had to have internal injuries after a fall like that, and broken bones. It looked at Paxton without fear, blinked once, and glanced away. Paxton wanted to do something for the squirrel but didn't know what. Clearly, it would die—that was a foregone conclusion. But it could lie here for hours, dying by inches. That was one of Paxton's worst-case battle scenarios, coming right behind the one where he was captured alive. Well, the rat had done that to him, hadn't it? But Paxton wasn't going to stand helplessly by and watch this squirrel linger through the other scenario. He picked it up in his left hand, the white fur of its belly upward. It looked back at him placidly and blinked again, seeming almost anesthetized. Tears gathered in his eyes as he looked down on it, realizing that they were both helpless, that neither of them could do a single thing to heal this small bit of life and make it viable again. There was no way to make the squirrel young or knit its bones, or coax its organs into wholeness again. All it could do was wait for death to take possession of its newest property. Well, Paxton couldn't stop the possession part, but he could do something about the waiting.

He stroked the squirrel's head lightly a few times with the tip of his index finger, then gently scratched it behind its ear. It looked up at him serenely. Then he took hold of the squirrel's head with his hand, and with a single swift motion wrung it from its body. The torso bled copiously onto the white snow when he dropped it. The red wetness at the base of the head he was holding made him think of the rose Henry always carried. He walked over to the gazebo. Henry's tomb figure held the granite bud, as it always would, but something was happening. He watched the stone flower begin to redden as the blood in Henry's effigy leeched up through the stem. A rich scarlet engorged the bud without haste and began to ooze out and form in droplets on the petals.

Paxton looked down at the bud in his own hand. "The rose bleeds us till we die," he murmured aloud, softly but quite distinctly. He looked back at the effigy, blood beginning to drip from Henry's rose. "And when we're dead, it bleeds us still."

One part of him concluded with calm logic that he was insane. Another part, grasping that there wasn't much time, was at once viscerally afraid, and he felt his testicles draw up and his scrotum contract and grow leathery. Still another part of him, sensing an ending scaled to the offense, resonated with a fierce and deliberate exaltation. But one more thing to do first—one last thing.

�

With self-pity and especially anger as the wallow of the evening, the vets' meeting had not been productive. Ned had tried with a question or two to push the group's focus toward future possibility, but for once they'd resisted that kind of aggressive leadership from one of their own. That function belonged to Hal, but in view of his pending departure he'd evidently stacked arms and lost interest. The two new men stood out because of their non-participation. They sat opposite each other in the circle, eyes constantly patrolling the entire group rather than focusing on the speaker. When a latecomer entered, the one with his back to the door jerked around in his chair and then deliberately subsided. At the same time, Ned glimpsed a sidearm under the windbreaker of the other one and everything became clear to him. They were cops waiting for the Ratman, and Hal was in on it. They'd have the outside covered as well.

That was when Ned had begun to throw questions at Hal, specific and openly barbed. No one else in the group seemed to have picked up on the presence of the cops, but the texture of Ned's questioning had an accusatory feel. Both the group and Hal detected it, and the psychologist responded with a guilty leap into the role of active facilitator. But Hal rang hollow and even suspicious after that, and the meeting came to a desultory end. When it was over, Ned confronted him. "Where the hell was your head tonight? Boston?"

"Made it easy for you to hijack the meeting, didn't it?"

"Or were you afraid the Ratman would actually show up and you'd wind up in the crossfire from those two cops?"

The color went out of Hal's face.

"If you were staying here, I'd throw you to the wolves." He realized Ned meant the other members of the group, which would completely destroy his usefulness to the center. "Go make lots of money," he said. "Die in your sleep." This last, as Hal knew very well, was a combat soldier's ultimate expression of contempt. Ned left him standing there and began circulating among the clusters of men remaining after the meeting.

It had not been a good day for Hal. He'd compromised his professional self twice in less than 12 hours, first by talking so freely about Paxton's habits and then by consenting to the subversion of the group, cracking its hermetic loyalty. There were differences between the bonding within the group and within a squad or platoon in combat, but they were still valid analogs, and Hal had knowingly set all that aside to get the detective off his back. Then, he'd been caught betraying the group, putting it at the service of outside interests. Some therapists, he knew, wouldn't find that disturbing under the circumstances, much less unethical, but Hal wasn't one of them. In a way, he wished he was.

Ned carried a great deal of personal authority among the clients, as the psychologists referred to the veterans, and the staff worked actively to stay on his good side. He was first among equals in a subgroup of vets that everyone called the Gun Oil Club, with qualification for membership being a failed suicide attempt. The name came from the taste of a pistol's muzzle, but any method would do. Ned, however, qualified on a literal basis. He had driven far out of the city one bleak winter day to a desolate section of forest, parked his car, and started walking. He sat down on a cushion of pine needles and leaned against a tree. After taking the magazine out of the automatic, he charged it with three rounds of explosive-head ammunition and replaced it. He took the weapon off safety, pulled the slide back, and stripped the first round into the chamber. Putting the muzzle in his mouth, he closed his eyes and squeezed the trigger. Nothing happened.

He sat for a long time then, the gun held loosely in his right hand. He mentally reviewed his actions in preparing the weapon and, satisfied he had made no mistakes, he aimed the piece at a tree ten feet away and again pulled the trigger. The sounds of the firing and the impact were simultaneous, and the ejected cartridge fell noiselessly on the pine needles. Where the round had struck, a rough, conical depression now gaped. The report's echo played back and forth among the trees.

He remained sitting there another long interval, dealing with issues of why. His cumulative experience during three tours in Vietnam would not allow him to conclude to a divinity. After what he'd done and seen, he most emphatically would not acknowledge, much less associate with, anything that launched and maintained a world such as this. Sitting under the gray overcast in the pine forest that day, he finally decided that he'd come to the attention of some sort of Power that was not capable of analysis. It was certainly not divine, probably not rational, and very likely depraved. And it wanted him to remain for some purpose, also not susceptible to reason. He didn't know why he'd been brought to this point or why he was supposed to stay, but he decided, for the time being at least, that he wouldn't resist.

Without a word, Ned passed Hal, who was waiting at the door to lock up. The psychologist was in his car before Ned reached his own at the other end of the parking lot, and was pulling into the street as Ned unlocked the door. He spotted a nondescript panel truck without markings parked and idling down the street. *The cops are still around.* He slid behind the wheel and started the engine.

"Ned, it's Paxton." The voice came from the floor of the back seat.

"Stay down. The cops are just down the street."

"I saw them on the way in."

Ned casually adjusted his gloves and fiddled with some buttons on the dash, then drove slowly to the street's edge, signaled his turn and merged into the sparse traffic. After a couple of minutes, he said, "They're not back there." Paxton joined him in the front seat.

"When did you eat last?"

After a pause, he said, "I'm not sure."

Ned picked up some fast food at a drive-through. They parked on a deserted side street and ate while they talked.

"I think it's time to move on."

They'd discussed the possibility before. He knew Paxton didn't mean to another city. Ned had concluded that Paxton had gone through more than enough in Nam. A major part of him was still stuck there and the way back out would be at least as painful as the going in. And it was entirely possible such an effort would prove futile anyway. When a dog has been hurt and is lingering in constant pain, we take it to the veterinarian, presumably out of love, and give it the gift of sleep. Surely, humans were worth the same loving and giving. Ned grasped Paxton's pain in terms of his own. It never even occurred to him to try and talk him out of it. "Don't forget what I told you. If you decide to use a pistol, through the mouth is best."

Paxton nodded and thought for a while, tearing the corner off a ketchup packet and squeezing the contents onto his french fries. "If I could remember the future," he said at last, "I could decide whether to stay." They smiled at that, but at the same time it made perfect sense to them both. "I live in borrowed clothes, you know? When something wears out, I have to spend a night in a shelter to get an issue of second-hand stuff. Somebody's old sweatshirt or some heavy socks with a hole that's not too big. My outsides aren't even mine any more. And it's too cold to go naked." Ned gave a snorty little laugh. Paxton grew more serious. "I was at the Garden all last night. Henry's gone, he's not coming back."

"What happened?"

"They called him back. I think because I killed M.J."

Ned knew he meant the cop. The story, with the Ratman's picture from basic training, was all over the papers and TV— although whatever resemblance that brand-new soldier had to this scraggly, bearded man was unvarnished coincidence. They ate in silence for a bit. Ned crumpled a burger wrapper and shoved it into the paper bag as Paxton resumed. "I got hold of a seed pod over there once. Early winter, right? Everything's dead. I open up that pod, it's dead too. The seeds are all dried up. How could anybody guess they'd sprout in the spring unless they'd seen it happen?" He paused, then looked at Ned. "What I'm scared of is, maybe I'm like a seed and all I have to do is buy a little more time, hang on a little longer. The snow will melt and with a little bit of sun, I'll come green again." He looked away and took a sip of coffee. "But when I think about it, it's really just a hope. Not even that—a wish. It'll never happen, not for me." He munched an apple cinnamon turnover, fine threads of steam rising from the freshly bitten end, then looked at Ned. "I need a twenty. I know you don't usually do that, but I need it." Without a word, Ned pulled out his wallet. *Probably not with a gun then. I wonder how?* He gave him two ten-dollar bills. *Means to an end.*

They sat together in silence for a few minutes, finishing their coffee. *The Ratman makes up his mind to kill himself while he's squeezing ketchup on his french fries. And while I help him decide, I keep one eye on the clock because I have to go to work tomorrow.* He thought about the hypothetical divinity of this real universe and was revolted all over again. He drank down the last of his coffee. "Where can I drop you?"

Paxton told him how to get in close to the rear of a small shopping mall without actually going into the parking lot. He'd shelter between a couple of dumpsters tonight. The metal would be cold, but he'd be out of the wind. He'd do his shopping when the stores opened the next morning.

They drove in silence to the drop-off point and then shook hands. Ned looked at him. "Good luck," he said simply. Paxton nodded, left the car and disappeared into the darkness.

※

He slept little that night, his shivering keeping him awake. When the sky began to lighten, he was grateful. *Fuck this arctic combat, I'm a jungle fighter.* He smiled at that and felt a bit better. His first glimpse of the sun at the horizon line told him it was just past 7:15 or so. He had almost three hours to wait for the stores to open. He was hungry and above all, he wanted to hold a cup of coffee in both hands for the sheer pleasure of the warmth. But he wasn't sure how much it would all cost and he wasn't going to spend a nickel till he'd bought everything else.

The backs of the dumpsters looked eastward, and he spent his time there facing the dawn. With no breeze, the sunshine began to warm him and he actually slept for an hour or so. The mall had only about a dozen shops, but he was able to get everything he needed, most of it at a crafts store, plus a breakfast croissant and a large coffee, which he loaded with sugar and cream. He wanted to sit at a table in the back, to be warm and indulge in the luxury of not thinking about anything—but if a cop came in on break, it would be all over.

Instead, he went back behind the dumpsters. When he finished eating, he carefully put his trash inside and then headed for the VFW. He reached the neighborhood club a half hour before noon. Except that he was a Vietnam vet and lived on the streets, the day manager, who had also done a tour in Nam, didn't know anything about Paxton. He would come in for a beer and a sandwich now and then when he had a few bucks. They talked briefly about the guy who'd killed the cop. When Paxton asked if he could catch a couple of hours' sleep in the storeroom and warm up, the manager had agreed and then turned to deal with his first lunch customers. Paxton thought the manager expected him to steal a can or two of food, probably even hoped he would. He smiled. *Not necessary.*

In the warm back room, he prepared his purchases and then got some more sleep. When he woke up, the day manager was serving the last few patrons. He put his preparation into his jacket pocket and eased out the back. It was a little after 2:00. He arrived at the convenience store about 2:30 and had to wait around the corner of the building for over an hour before he got what he was looking for. A paunchy guy, early 40s, dressed casually but expensively, tooled into a parking slot in a cherry red BMW and hurried into the store, leaving the engine running. In seconds, Paxton was around the corner and into the driver's seat. He dropped it into reverse and was wheeling out of the lot and into the street as the guy came out the door. He watched him in the mirror for a second, shaking a pack of cigarettes angrily over his head and mouthing selected obscenities.

He headed straight for the interstate that ran across the river. The guy would be phoning the cops right now on the store's pay phone, so there wasn't much time. He checked the dash—a quarter of a tank of gas. It would be enough. He took the on-ramp and merged with the traffic, then slipped over to the far left lane and into the middle of half-a-dozen cars that were running ten miles over the limit. If they came on a speed trap, the cop probably wouldn't pursue anybody in the clump. There was a good chance he wouldn't even see the BMW's license number.

Prophetic. When they topped the next rise, they were looking at a squad car on the left shoulder, with a radar unit clamped to the rear window. Ignoring Paxton's best-case scenario, he kicked on his lights and initiated pursuit. When the two cars behind him moved right a couple of lanes and the squad car stayed with him, Paxton knew who he wanted. *No more cherry red BMWs, thanks.*

They passed over a full interchange, and a standard break in the metal highway divider was coming up fast. Paxton slid onto the left shoulder, the cop right behind him. As he got near the gap in the divider, Paxton stood on the brakes and whipped left through the opening, ripping the right side against the divider from headlights to rear bumper. He thought about the BMW's owner. *Maybe now he'll quit smoking.* The cop swung frantically back out into the traffic lane, narrowly missing the BMW's fender, and hurtled past the opening. He then swung back onto the left shoulder, braking to a halt, and began backing up at speed.

Paxton had no choice. He floored it, swung at once into a U-turn in the face of the oncoming traffic, and headed for the far right lane. He heard the screech of brakes and the grind of metal on metal behind him. For an instant, he saw the cop in his mirror, now on Paxton's side of the divider but waiting for a gap in the traffic. He started into his own U-turn as Paxton took the off-ramp. At the bottom, he pushed straight through a red light and turned left under the highway overpass. Twenty yards later, he made another immediate left turn onto the opposite on-ramp. He ended up back on the interstate, going in the same direction he was traveling when the speed trap interrupted him. He didn't see the cop at the underpass before he went back up on the highway, which meant the cop didn't see him make his move, so Paxton had probably bought himself another few minutes. It was all he wanted. Three more exits remained before the highway reached the river. He got off at the next, one exit sooner than he'd planned.

He threaded through cross-town traffic, heading toward the bridge of his choice. Built right after the turn of the century, the McKinley was one of the few major spans left in the United States on which vehicle and railroad traffic still shared the same roadbed. It was three lanes wide, westbound traffic having one lane, eastbound having two—except that the outside lane for eastbound traffic was also the bed for the railroad track going across the bridge. When a train was crossing in either direction, there was unequivocally only one lane for eastbound vehicles, the bridge's middle lane.

Two blocks short of the McKinley approach, another squad car caught sight of him and started its pursuit with lights and siren. Weaving in and out of traffic, it took him just under a minute to travel the two blocks. At the first cross street, he narrowly missed plowing broadside into another squad car just entering the intersection. As he finally achieved the bridge approach, he had two cop cars in pursuit, one on his bumper, the other trying to get around him on his left to cut him off. When he lurched wildly at it to prevent being passed, the car behind tried to come around on his right. He swung back over to block that and as he hugged the guard rail for a second, the other car pulled abreast of him on his left. Now, over water, they rounded the last bend of the approach onto the bridge proper. Then, deep and solid below the shrilling of the sirens, he heard the blast of a diesel horn and looked up to see a freight train rumbling toward him at speed.

Instantly, along with the sirens and the diesel's horn, came the sound of the freight train's brakes as the engine and the BMW sped toward each other. Even though the train was moving at a safe rate for the bridge, it would take it more than a quarter of a mile to stop, and Paxton was doing almost 60. He stomped on the brake pedal, both squad cars staying right with him. He jammed it into park and had just enough time to roll across and out the passenger door, and then the engine slammed into the BMW. It crumpled the front end and stood the car on its head, ramming its underside into the police car behind it and grinding the two together just as the cop bailed out the driver's side. The scream of metal scouring metal joined the general din and was continuous, as the engine tumbled and ground the two cars together. The span between the bridge abutments shook, the surface undulating as if in a wind. It would take the train at least another 30 seconds or so to stop. For that brief time his side of the bridge, four feet wide from train to railing, was Paxton's alone. He was exactly where he wanted to be, and the time left, though short, was enough.

He walked another ten feet along the bridge, noticing the lights of a barge or two down in the gathering twilight. As a gap between freight cars thundered past, he caught sight of one of the cops keeping pace with him. He was there again at the next opening, waiting till he could get safely onto the other side. Paxton smiled. *You're too late.*

He strode over to one of the bridge uprights and steadied himself on it with his left hand. As he climbed up onto the guard rail, another vacant space slid past behind him. He took what he'd prepared out of his right jacket pocket, holding on to it tightly. Then, he searched his memory for the day he sat in the door of the chopper and used insect repellent to flush the leeches off his body and out into the air. Found it. Searched for the feeling that said it was time to stand up and walk away, time at last to push the wind aside. Found it. Another empty gap flashed past behind him as he let go of the upright and stepped off into space, wishing above all that he could have kept the rat inside and taken it with him.

He sensed his body turning in ways he didn't want, like an Olympic diver going wrong. He was falling nearly horizontal to the river, rotating toward the sinking crescent of sun, and then his head smashed against the top of a massive stone abutment. With his skull fractured and neck broken, his body spun in a new direction until a wire, strung taut beneath the bridge, caught his outstretched right hand and severed it swiftly and cleanly from the rest of him. It fell free into the broad expanse of darkening river, while his body shattered itself on the hatch cover of a passing barge and lay still.

Six days later, Paxton was interred in the national cemetery at Jefferson Barracks, high up on the western bluffs of the river. After a brief hue and cry about how a cop killer would dishonor the other vets buried there, Hal entered the public debate. He pointed out that what Paxton went through in combat had left him capable of what he'd done, and that his awards for valorous acts performed and wounds received more than qualified him for an honored place of rest. He postponed his departure for Boston to be at the interment.

He exchanged a few words with Paxton's grandmother in her wheelchair and with a young woman holding the hand of her small son. He wondered if Paxton was the father. Ned and a few of the other group members stood in the bitter cold as well. Hal thought about Paxton's Silver Star and the other awards. Shouldn't they go on the doctor's certificate as cause of death? But no, he decided. Much too melodramatic for an emotionally exhausted age. Year by year, we've been disabused of our ideals, often violently, and what remains as sole defense against our fears and self-doubts is a weary, brittle cynicism, which we both disbelieve and deeply resent, and which itself never fails to spill blood.

At taps, most of the men placed their hands over their hearts and one or two saluted. Ned just stood quietly, hands in his pockets, thinking of the last time he saw Paxton alive, of ketchup on french fries and the smell of hot apples and cinnamon, and wondered what else the Power had kept him there to witness.

The day after the funeral, just below Jefferson Barracks, a fisherman snagged the severed hand. The medical examiner duly pried open its fingers and pulled out the sodden piece of cloth. Paxton had selected his materials with care. None of the dyes had bled, even after days in the river. Below the crude rendering of the Stars and Stripes, his message was clearly legible:

I am an American soldier. I do not speak your language. Misfortune forces me to seek your help. Please take me to one who will care for me and restore me to my people.

ACKNOWLEDGMENTS

Many people helped in the writing of this book over the years, too many to list in full. To all of them I express my gratitude. Still, I have to thank the following: Steve Acai, who served in Graves Registration in Nam, and told me how it was; John Hunt, who before he became an M.D. was a Navy Corpsman with the Marines; Larry L. King, a writer always at work, who mentored me by words, example, and letters of introduction; Barbara and Ed Whitmarsh, first for *Incoming!,* which would be more than enough by itself, and then for publishing in it an excerpt from *Blood Chit;* all the nurses who served in Nam, and especially those who wrote honest-to-the-bone memoirs so we'd know you don't have to carry a rifle to suffer battle trauma; Jay Fisher, who worked as an EMT, saving many lives in the process, and who described what happens; Terry Paiste, who encouraged *Blood Chit* from its very beginnings; all the members of Playwrights Anonymous who read drafts of *Blood Chit* across time—you know who you are; and Nicole J. Burton—Nicki, the sine qua non lady: no Nicki, no *Blood Chit.*

And, of course, Katy.

Herman Wouk, in a note to *The Caine Mutiny,* took pains to distinguish between the fictional, and insane, Captain Queeg, and the two destroyer captains he actually served under during World War II. Both officers were decorated for valor. In *Blood Chit,* I write about a fictitious VA psychologist whose career comes before his patients. In real life, I worked with a psychologist at a VA storefront clinic, and his efforts helped me come to terms in absolutely vital ways with my Vietnam experience. I will always be grateful to him.

✱

Other characters in this novel redeem their own Blood Chits. Captain Bonner, Garrett Prue, Ken Janowitz, Carmen Griggs, and Al Gomez all deal with what they experienced in Vietnam. Their stories are at **www.gradysmithbooks.com.**

CPSIA information can be obtained at www.ICGtesting.com
Printed in the USA
BVOW012126150412

287701BV00005B/2/P

9 780979 899225